A HEART THAT LIES

Jackie O'Hara has been in a race against time. Terminally ill, she's determined to make peace with her estranged brother, yet there is just one problem — first, she must find him. Meanwhile, Danny is being chased by the Russian Mafia who want him dead, and Interpol, who need him to testify against mob boss Dmitri Kaslov. That makes Jackie a target as well, because they all hope she will lead them straight to him . . .

STEVE HAYES
AND
ANDREA WILSON

◆

A HEART
THAT LIES

LINFORD
Leicester

First published in Great Britain

First Linford Edition
published 2013

Names, characters and incidents in this book are
fictional, and any resemblance to actual events,
locales, organizations, or persons,
living or dead is purely coincidental.

A catalogue record for this book is available
from the British Library.

ISBN 978–1–4448–1618–1

Published by
F. A. Thorpe (Publishing)
Anstey, Leicestershire

Set by Words & Graphics Ltd.
Anstey, Leicestershire
Printed and bound in Great Britain by
T. J. International Ltd., Padstow, Cornwall

This book is printed on acid-free paper

Part One

1

The customs official glanced at the passport in front of him. He ran his eyes over it briefly before looking up at me to compare the face before him with the photo. He couldn't possibly have spent more than two seconds analyzing the two before proceeding with his questions. I was beginning to think I'd wasted my time and money procuring the fake. I was apparently boring him — just another wealthy tourist arriving by private jet into Nice, France.

'Reason for visit?'

I had a pair of over-sized sunglasses resting on the top of my head keeping my formerly auburn hair out of my face. I'd visited Garren's salon, back home in Manhattan, before chartering the flight. Kirk did whatever Kirk does and got me the appointment. He was more than happy to help me, thinking my sudden interest in a $400 cut and color must mean I was looking to put my Danny chasing, mobster escaping, past behind me. He was so pleased that I was looking to spend some time pampering myself. I wanted him to believe I was going to relax and focus on my health. He didn't realize I'd taken my red hair several shades lighter, chartered a plane, purchased a fake passport, and left the country. I left NYC as Jackie O'Hara and landed in Nice, Jackie Proctor. I didn't intend to keep the alias for long, just to get me off the grid and out of the States. I didn't want anyone to know I'd skipped town.

'Vacation. Just a much needed vacation.' I looked straight at the clerk with a tired, jet-lagged smile and tried to emit the lie with a tone that matched his and conveyed an equal amount of boredom. It was a difficult task as I'm not a liar, at least not a good one, and my heart was beating in a wild erratic rhythm.

I'm not a deceptive person. I despise people who lack the courage and confidence to be truthful, but my current situation has led me to see the value of duplicity. It's almost an art form really.

I've discovered a new appreciation for my brother, Danny, whose lying, cheating, self-serving ways, landed me in this situation. Danny's a master deceiver. His work could be cataloged in a museum for world-class cons, if such a place existed.

To be fair, I can't really blame him for my situation. He didn't ask me to find him. Quite the opposite, he's furious that I've gotten involved. Sadly, he thinks I'm chasing him because he stole a hundred thousand dollars from me. He's wrong.

He's not the only one who's angry about my involvement. I've managed to make a long list of people mad. Every law enforcement agency from the NYPD to Interpol, my ex-husband Kirk, and the Russian Mafia, is praying for my resolve to diminish so I'll stay out of their way. Or in Kirk's case, just stay where he knows I'm safe. But if I was tenacious before, when I understood risk, you should see me now. Now I view risk as a conceptual luxury for those who have a future. I'm dying anyway — so what do I have to lose.

I was diagnosed with Leukemia right

before my brother fled the U.S. I tried to tell him about my diagnosis, hoping it would be the catalyst needed to get him off drugs and out of trouble. Unfortunately, I was too late. I caught up to him right about the time he started being shot at by Kaslov's men. And he, being paranoid, actually believed I'd brought them there, set him up. So now I chase. I've chased him from Harlem, to the beaches of Ipanema, Tokyo and now the South of France. I'm determined to heal this relationship before I die and I don't care what continent I have to travel to, to do it.

Danny and I have not had an easy life. Both our parents died when we were teens and it's been just the two of us. I did the best I could to become a surrogate mom to him, but I wasn't equipped to handle the choices he'd come to make or the addictions he'd become a slave to. Eventually I had to let him lead the life he was committed to living and I moved on with mine. I started a successful ad agency in Manhattan, and married Kirk Harmon. The former worked out beautifully, the latter — not so much.

Kirk and I would be perfect for each other, if only we were both completely different people. I've already told you how I feel about deception. It's an art form I despise. Kirk, however, decorates his house with it. I was never able to get the smell of dirty money or cheap perfume out of his clothes. And rather than continue to ruin both our lives, we decided to tap out and leave the ring as friends rather than enemies.

Thump. The sound of the clerk's stamp calmed my heart and brought a genuine smile to my face. '*Bienvenue à Nice.*'

'*Merci.*'

2

In my former life, the one I can barely recall, I loved to I travel. And walking through this airport I could easily have fooled myself into believing I was actually on vacation.

The facility caters to the wealthy. Private planes fly in at all times of the day and night carrying the world's elite. During the renowned Cannes Film Festival, it's heavily trafficked by celebrities. The airport knows who its clients are and it serves them well. The shops and restaurants are first class and the staff minds its own business.

I walked through the terminal slowly, admiring the artwork, pausing at the aquarium. I wasn't in a hurry. I've learned the more inconspicuous you try to appear the more conspicuous you become. I strolled around in knee-high, stiletto boots, and a classic Burberry trench coat, opened to reveal a tight, belted black dress. I looked hot. I looked like someone who wanted to be noticed. No one who is looking for Danny even knows I've left the States. I'm the hunter this time. I wanted to have a pulse on the chatter floating around and to do that I needed to make some new friends. I was dressed for the occasion.

I stepped into one of the restaurant bars looking forward to a Vodka Martini and an opportunity to watch. I like to study. I watched the travelers arriving and knew I'd see some of them again, at the poolside, a bar, a restaurant. It's just the way it is when you travel. Being February, the crowd arriving was a little mellower than what you'd see in late spring or summer, when socialites arrive wearing sheer blouses over tiny camisoles and more jewelry than would seem necessary for drinking by the pool. Now it's middle-aged couples making their way through the airport. The women, like the socialites, wearing more jewelry than would seem necessary, but also dressed in Chanel ready-to-wear as they follow their Louis Vuitton luggage, being pulled by the porter, through the terminal. These are the people I expect. These are the people I see while sitting at the bar with my drink. The more I see what I expect the quicker I'll recognize someone who doesn't belong. I know I belong. Kirk and I were one of these couples. I know how to fit in here.

Kirk, God bless him, is the reason I'm here. He doesn't know it but it was his tip that brought me here. I've long suspected his ties to Kaslov but he's always denied it. I don't think he has any real connection to the hit out on Danny, but I'm certain he knows more than he's letting on. There have always been too many unexplained coincidences. If I pressed hard enough I'm sure I could find out everything I wanted to know about his Mafia ties, but the less I know the safer I am. I know he'd never want to put me in danger and I wouldn't want to give Kaslov any excuse to knock him off, or me for that matter. I'm not a threat to anyone at this point. I'm a connection to Danny that they'd like to keep alive.

There's always the hope he'll reach out to me.

On the day I found out about Danny's location, I had surprised Kirk at his office. I know men don't like to be surprised at work in the middle of the day, but I can be delightfully annoying in that way. It was a point of contention in our marriage and now I do it just to be a nuisance. When we were married it was the only way to get time together. Now I do it to see what I can find out. I also enjoy seeing him get flustered when I catch him flirting with his secretary, Jeanine. And yes, she's every bit the cliché you're envisioning — pencil skirts that appear to have been stitched onto her body, heels that could moonlight as stilts, and lips that remain sealed. She's the perfect secretary for a secretive man with a wandering eye. On this particular day Jeanine was away from her desk. So, unfortunately for him, there was no one to announce my arrival. I didn't hesitate to eavesdrop at the door when I heard him on the phone, which wasn't difficult since he was shouting.

'Just take care of it.' He slammed his hand on his desk. 'I don't care how. I need him off my docket of concern. The French Riviera is not a difficult place to track down a two-bit drug addict on the run. Do it.'

At that moment I walked in. I needed to see what his reaction would be. It's hard to recover when you've been caught, even when you're as polished as Kirk. He started shouting before even looking up, clearly expecting Jeanine.

'Jeanine! Never . . . ' He looked up and froze, not for long, but I saw it. 'Irish, for Chr— ' he stopped himself from lashing out at me. 'What are you doing here? Where's Jeanine?'

'Ohhh I don't know,' I said breezily, 'I was just in the neighborhood. Who was that? Everything ok?'

'Nothing, nothing.' He took the blue-tooth from his ear, straightened his tie and smoothed back his dark hair. He was aging beautifully, just the right amount of gray adding wisdom and experience to his hair and sexy creases around his eyes suggesting a man that smiled often. 'Just some . . . uh . . . pro-bono work.

'Really? Pro-bono?' As I said, I don't really know what Kirk does in his job as 'a lawyer-of-sorts', the career title he often gives himself; he could be telling the truth, but my intuition was telling me otherwise. He looked caught when I walked in the door and his behavior was giving off signals that shouted cover-up.

He came around the desk and put his hands on my arms and kissed my cheek. He was dangerously close and looked me straight in the eye. 'Don't look so surprised. I've been known to perform a random act of kindness now and then.' His voice was low and seductive.

I maintained his eye contact and he maintained his grasp on my arms. 'Random huh? I've never known you to do anything without calculation.'

'How about marrying you?'

'You got me there. We both could have used a little more thought before making that decision.'

He dropped his head and let out a little laugh, the spell broken, the moment passed. It was intimate moments like that that got us down to the altar. Back then we didn't know the difference between good chemistry and love. 'Well, it wasn't all bad,' he said, as he walked over to the bar. Whatever was to come next would be the deciding factor for me. If the phone call had really been about a client, the conversation would have dropped right there and we would have moved on to inconsequential aspects of our lives, thrown a few verbal jabs, shared a pitcher of martinis and then I'd be off. But if he continued to try and cover his tracks I'd know the two-bit drug-addict in question was Danny.

'Yeah,' he said as if we were still talking about his phone call. 'I've got this friend whose son is a total screw-up . . . ' And there it was, the continuation of the story. If only he'd known when to shut up. Apparently they don't teach you that in 'lawyer-of-sorts' school. I don't even know what he said next, it didn't matter. I knew he was lying and all I could think about was getting to France to find Danny.

'Hey you, you still with me?'

'Sorry, I was, uh, just pre-occupied with some agency stuff.'

'Irish, I thought you were done with that. You need to focus on your health. You can't be worrying about the agency anymore, that's Dana's headache now, you sold it to her, let her take care of the problems. You've got enough on your plate.'

'You're right, I know.' I was lying of course. Dana had been running the agency for months without a single issue. 'I couldn't agree with you more. I think I'll go treat myself to a day at the salon.'

'Brilliant. Let me call in a favor, I'll get you into Garren's.' He was quite pleased with himself.

'Perfect.' I was quite pleased too.

3

I finished my drink and left the airport bar. I walked through the halls planning to catch a shuttle to my hotel but was caught off guard when I noticed a simple sign hanging above a glass-enclosed reception area. The sign written in both French and English read: *Espace de Prières*, space of prayer. I was intrigued and stood for a moment looking through the glass doors. There were three simple wooden doors that led to prayer rooms for passengers to spend time in meditation. I have never been a religious person, but curiosity got the better of me. I opened the outer glass door that led into the reception area. At the moment I stepped in one of the prayer room doors opened. A man stepped out crossing himself as he closed the door behind him. He was tall, at least 6'2", bright blue eyes with dark hair cut short. He was impeccably dressed in a dark suit and recently polished shoes. I felt a twinge of shame for checking him out as he left a place of worship, but he was impossibly beautiful. He passed me as I stood by the front door and nodded in acknowledgement of my presence but didn't smile or speak. He was solemn and reverent and I felt further chastised for my irreverence. I waited for a few seconds before walking into the room he'd left. In stark contrast to the rest of the airport's cold glass and steel modern design, this room was warm and understated in beige tones and soft lighting. A wooden cross, softly lit from behind, hung on the wall near a waist high wooden podium. The large flat surface of the podium held a black leather Bible, which lay open to the book of Ecclesiastes. I stood over it and read a few lines: 'So I hated life, for the work which had been done under the sun was grievous to me; because everything is futility and striving after the wind.'

I couldn't disagree with those words and found myself wondering if the man who'd been here before me was reading Solomon's cryptic observation of the meaning of life, or if he'd just been in here to pray and spend time with God; both options were foreign concepts to me. I sat down on a small tufted stool that looked more like an ottoman than a seat. It was peaceful in there. For a moment I felt as though the never-ending thoughts about life and death, Danny, failed relationships — the futility of life, as Solomon said — cleared from my mind. I briefly let myself enjoy the rest but not for long. 'Get up Ms. O,' I said to the empty room, 'you've got work to do.'

* * *

My shuttle to the hotel was empty, not a single passenger beside myself and I was grateful. I didn't have it in me to fake enthusiasm for the shallow conversation travelers have with one another about where they're from, where they're staying, have you been here before, blah, blah, blah. I laid my head back on the window of the van and felt every bit like a woman who needed a vacation. But before I could get too comfortable the shuttle driver began to get chatty. In good English with a heavy French accent he started asking too many questions. Why would a beautiful woman choose the winter to vacation in the Riviera, when a bikini wouldn't be necessary? Why was I traveling alone? Would I be attending the Mimosa festival in Mandelieu-Napoule, oh I just must, it's charming. When I closed my eyes and tilted my head back he finally got the idea that I wasn't interested in a conversation.

Winter in the Riviera is quiet. The days are mild but an early setting sun leads to cold nights. The day was winding down and I was tired. A long flight, a surge of adrenalin at the fear of being arrested for a fraudulent passport, and acknowledgement of the task that was ahead of me, had taken its toll. Life had spun out of the real reason. I knew I just needed to recharge.

As we turned a corner the hotel came into sight. It was imposing. Carved into a cliff, it was a semi-private resort with a 180-degree view of the Mediterranean. From the shuttle it seemed to be floating in the sea between Monaco and Nice. It had been the vacation home for a family of Russian Royals in the late 1800s. The designers who had transformed it into a hotel had taken care to retain the palatial look of the mansion's four stories with white palisades on every level of the pale yellow palace. As the shuttle passed through the iron gates I envisioned the castle as it must have appeared when princes and princesses danced in their gowns and robes, drunk on spirits, joyfully celebrating their station.

I was led to my room by an uninterested bellman. He nodded at my luggage, picked up my bags and started walking toward the suites. He didn't attempt to make small talk or make a speech about the hotel's amenities. I sensed he'd been trained to protect the privacy and anonymity of the clients. I liked it.

He opened the door to my suite, set my bags down and stood by the door while I looked around briefly. He nodded, and then was gone. 'I think that is the beginning of a beautiful friendship,' I said, thinking aloud, as I crossed the simple, elegant room toward my private balcony.

The Mediterranean Sea sparkled as though a fairy had sprinkled her dust all over the surface, the sun sharing its last few rays of the day with her. I leaned against the concrete parapet and took a deep breath, feeling the tension leave my shoulders. My thoughts traveled to Danny and me as children, playing hide and seek. He always won. He could stay hidden for hours if he had to. 'Well, Danny, where are you hiding this time?' I asked the view. 'Come out, come out wherever you are.'

4

My eyes opened slowly as I processed my surroundings. I'd slept well, well enough to not remember my dreams. With my head still propped against the pillow I noticed the white room with pops of color provided by jewel toned turquoise pillows and vases. It looked as though the sea had sprayed a few drops of water throughout the room.

I began moving around the suite, brewing tea, setting out clothes — preparing for the day as though I had a plan. The intensity and resolve I'd felt upon my arrival in the airport seemed to be more difficult to conjure up now. But regardless, it's my nature to take action. Procrastination and indifference have never been my weaknesses. I'd rather fake enthusiasm and decisiveness than succumb to uselessness. Even faking it can lead to a sudden wave of direction and fervor.

I slipped into my skinny black jeans, boots, and fitted, white, button-down blouse and headed to the lounge for some breakfast. I was directed to a small, two-top, glass table and seated in a white leather chair. The restaurant was not busy. I ordered black coffee, a croissant and a bowl of strawberries in cream.

I sipped my coffee and looked out over the hotel grounds. The landscape seemed to be dropping off right into the ocean. I watched people inside the restaurant enjoy the start of their day. Since my CML diagnosis, Danny's disappearance, and my subsequent run-ins with Dmitri Kaslov and his thugs, I've found myself taking pleasure in the mundaneness of other peoples' lives. My life had become anything other than mundane.

Across the dining room a young couple sat at a small table, seated across from one another. The woman was striking in an I've-spent-thousands-of-dollars-on-this-face-and-body kind of way. Her lips had been plumped to an unnatural size. Her breasts, which had also been clearly enhanced, were barely covered by the plunging neckline of her blouse. Her hair had been blown-out pin-straight, and subjected to an unnatural amount of heat from a flat iron, there wasn't a wisp of her platinum floss out of line.

Her swollen, raspberry-painted lips were parted in a childish pout and she was whining about something in Russian. I instantly focused my attention toward the window, pretending to be fascinated by the palatial gardens, while I listened intently. All I heard was something about Mandelieu-Napoule.

I didn't get a look at her companion's face but after a few minutes of her tantrum she'd obviously gotten her way because she eventually wiggled out of her seat, plopped herself on his lap, and threw her arms around his neck. *Sucker*, I thought. I wasn't the only one to notice, they were the hit of the breakfast crowd. They got up to leave the restaurant and I busied myself in my bag, not that I was in any danger of being noticed, she was draped all over him as they left and his eyes never left her chest.

As they walked out I remembered the

shuttle driver's insistence that I check out the Mimosa Festival in Mandelieu-Napoule. Suddenly a festival sounded like a lovely idea.

★　★　★

I had a car delivered to the hotel and made my way to the festival. The scent of mimosas brought a sense of playfulness to the air. The town was in full celebration mode. The yellow clusters of mimosa glowed and hung proudly on the green stalks, basking in their moment to shine. I found myself walking through a variety of street artists and musicians, all celebrating the sweetly fragrant flower. The glorious bloom had brought a great deal of income to the area when it was introduced in the 19th century, and now a forest of mimosa trees spread from the village. I looked for the couple from the restaurant but I couldn't see them anywhere. You can call it paranoia, sixth sense, whatever, but I knew they were tied to Kaslov, she was a mobster's girl if I'd ever seen one. I was hoping they'd lead me to Danny.

I spent an hour making my way through the crowd. They wouldn't be difficult to spot. They were not the type to blend into the background. As I was scanning the crowd I saw him. Only, it was the wrong him. Instead of a Russian thug, my eyes landed on the man from the airport prayer room.

He was talking to an elderly woman who looked like she'd been attending this festival for a lifetime. He put a hand gently on her shoulder and pointed out one of the floats passing by in a parade. I caught myself staring and he caught me too. He turned his head and made eye contact. But just as quickly, turned his head in the other direction. I was instantly drawn to him and instantly suspicious of his presence. Like I said, it's not unusual to run into the same people more than once when traveling, but I'm not used to running into the ones you hope to see again. I'm not one to believe in coincidences, serendipity is for the naïve. But I was certain, whether friend or foe, I needed to get closer to him. He was dressed casually in dark jeans, a black T-shirt, which lay flat against his stomach, and a large silver watch that drew my eye to his toned forearms. He had a black messenger bag slung across his body, the strap crossing over his chest. He was fit, athletic-looking and seemed confident.

I watched him help the elderly woman to a car that was waiting for her. He waved as she was driven away and then turned toward a concession. I took the opportunity to follow and stood behind him in line for wine.

'Cinsault veuillez,' he said, to the girl smiling sweetly in the booth. Big plumes of mimosa draped down the tent and several bottles of wine decorated a table behind her. She turned and poured a luscious garnet-colored liquid into a glass.

'Would you recommend it?' I asked, getting his attention.

He turned and smiled casually.

'Indeed. The grape does well in this region.' I was shocked at his British accent, his French sounded perfect and I'd just assumed he was a native. He turned back to the girl who'd returned with his glass. 'Deux,' he said, holding up two fingers. He turned back to me. 'Allow me,' he said, handing me his glass while she turned and poured another.

'Merci,' I said with a nod of my head. Normally, my pride would not allow me to accept such a presumptuous gesture, but I got the sense refusing would mystify him. He didn't seem like the type of man who received many rejections. He took his glass, paid, and pointed toward the side of the tent to a group of tables shaded by mimosa trees.

I took a seat across from him at a small, wrought-iron table. 'Cheers,' I said.

'Yes,' he said, as he raised his glass to brush the side of mine.

He reached his hand across the table. 'Martin.'

'Jackie. It's a pleasure to meet you. Thanks for the wine, it's lovely.'

He nodded. 'Is this your first time to the Festival?' he asked.

'Yes, I've actually never been to the Riviera this time of year. It's beautiful. You?'

He smiled broadly, his jawline strengthening with the movement. 'No, I come every year.'

'Really?' The festival was delightful but not spectacular enough to draw someone every year.

He laughed at my question. 'Yes, really.'

'I'm sorry, I don't mean to offend, but why?' He took a sip of wine. 'To see the glorious mimosa in bloom of course.'

I have a tendency to get sarcastic and even a bit cagey when . . . well let's face it, when I'm breathing, so I took immediate pleasure in identifying the sarcasm in his voice.

'I see,' I said, smiling over my glass.

'And also to have a glass of wine with a lovely stranger,' he said, gesturing toward me with his glass.

'Oh. Well, I'm glad I could help you in your annual mission.'

'Yes, it was rather kind of you to help.'

He continued to sip his wine while I stared at him with a raised eyebrow, letting him know that I actually wanted an answer.

'Well, I can see nothing gets past you, you must be a detective of sorts.'

'Of sorts. Yes,' I said, wondering if he realized how close to the truth he'd landed.

'My grandmother is from this village. She actually still lives here. And my mother was raised here.'

'So you come to visit your grandmother?'

'Yes, adorable isn't it?'

Perfect. He was absolutely, self-deprecatingly, perfect. So of course I became immediately suspicious. *I'll have to keep this one close*, I thought.

'That's very sweet. So do you wheel your poor grandmother out here every year just to entice lovely strangers to drink a glass of wine with you?'

'Ah, yes, your exceptional deductions have caught me.' He leaned toward me and waved me forward, glancing from side to side. 'You see,' he said in a whisper, 'Grand-mère is bait.' His delivery was dry and clever. He leaned back in his chair, and flaunted a satisfied smile. 'No, it's quite the opposite really. My mother ran off with my father, to his hometown, London,' he said, gesturing toward himself as if to say that explained the accent. 'They were young and in love. Mother was determined to follow Father. Her parents were against it, but seeing they were no match for true love,' he said with a slight lilt and sarcasm in his voice, acknowledging the sickly sweetness of young love, 'they eventually consented. Grand-mère, however, made my mother swear she'd bring her children — which ended up being child, only me I'm afraid — every year for the festival. Grand-mère loves this festival, she won the annual beauty contest when she was young, she's quite passionate about it.'

I laughed at the notion of his dear grandmother prancing around in the beauty contest. I felt myself relaxing when a voice in my head brought tension to my shoulders. *Trust no one.* His story was endearing. A little too endearing, almost as if rehearsed. The thought must have clouded my face because he noticed the change.

'Everything okay?'

I recovered quickly and painted the smile back on my face. 'Yes, of course. I was just picturing Grand-mère in a swim suit.'

'Oh please,' he said, 'you mustn't.' He shook his head as if trying to get the thought out of his mind. 'It was all much more civilized back then.' We both laughed and continued to sip our wine. We sat quietly for longer than is normally comfortable for me. I tend to be hyper — conversational lulls are not my thing. He seemed to feel no pressure to fill the space between us with nervous banter. There wasn't anything nervous about him. We watched the parade of floats travel by. He never looked at his watch, checked his phone, or looked around, suspicious of those nearby. He was simply enjoying the moment. *What is that like?* I wondered. It had been so long since I just relaxed in a moment. I've spent the last several months running, chasing, and trying my best to ignore my diagnosis. So much so, that I've been frightened of a quiet moment. If left alone too long, I start filling the quiet space with my own voice talking to myself.

Eventually the glasses were emptied. We were faced with a choice, go our separate ways or make dinner plans. I wasn't sure which I wanted more. I couldn't trust him, even though I was fairly certain he wasn't with Kaslov. But Kaslov wasn't my only concern.

'Well, Jackie, have you plans for dinner?'

'No, Martin, I do not.'

'Good, because you know so much about my Grand-mère and I know nothing about yours.'

'Oh, well, she's just delightful, let's get dinner so I can tell you all about her.'

5

The dinner conversation covered everything from favorite places in the world to wake up — Martin: any exotic beach, me: Manhattan — to what color most dominated our closets — black, on both accounts. The more wine we drank the looser the conversation became. However, it was becoming obvious that both of us were avoiding any conversation that led to more identifying topics, such as careers, family, and associates. And since my radar is never down, I decided it was time to stop having fun and figure out who this guy was. Even though part of me, a large part of me, wanted to forget my responsibilities, my reason for being there, and just relax in a romantic vacation fling. Kirk was right, I needed a break, and a handsome man and lots of wine were winning me over.

We had driven to the small restaurant in separate cars. I felt safer knowing I had my car. I was determined to sleep in my own bed, tucked away safely in my hotel. We drove just a few miles from the festival, my Audi rental trailing his smoky-black BMW with blacked-out windows. It wasn't a rental and I found it hard to believe he was borrowing it from Grand-mère. I didn't know what to think of it and just filed it away in my mind under interesting.

We made our way down a small cobbled stone alleyway lined with arched entryways, each leading to small homes, and one that led to a quaint little restaurant. Eight rustic, wooden tables, each with a jug of wine serving as a centerpiece, filled the small space. The stone lined walls were unadorned. The only décor necessary was the aroma and laughter coming from the kitchen. When we entered, a young man, who couldn't have been far beyond 18 years old, came and greeted Martin with a loud 'Martin!' and a big manly, clenched fist hug and a kiss on either cheek. They exchanged a few words in French before Martin introduced me. I learned his name was

Talon and his parents owned the little restaurant attached to their home. Talon tipped his head to me, seated us, and poured us each a glass of wine from the jug on the table.

'Hope you like the house red,' Martin said, with a smile and a little wink that made me think this might be a test to see how high I registered on the maintenance scale. I didn't have to fake it, not that I would have, because it was perfect and I enjoyed glass after glass.

'You look deliciously relaxed Jackie.'

'I am. A little too relaxed probably.'

'That sounds like Manhattan talking. Isn't tranquility what the vacationer sets out to find?'

'Who said I was on vacation?' I said, with a drowsy, wine-induced smile.

'Oh? Business?'

Here was the second time since our meeting that a decision had to be made. It was stupid of me to allow the night to get this far. Did I divulge my true reason for being here? Or concoct a tale? I didn't really know who this guy was or what he did for a living. He could be looking for

Danny too, for a very different reason. I was caught between paranoia and lust, focus and exhaustion. Not every good-looking guy who's interested in me is looking to kill Danny, or maybe they are. I couldn't help but think he did remind me a bit of . . .

'James Bond.'

'I'm sorry,' Martin said looking confused. 'Did you just say James Bond?'

I'd spoken my thoughts out loud and laughed, slightly embarrassed. 'I was just thinking this whole scene reminds me of a James Bond film.'

'I like it. Let's play Bond,' he said, leaning in, taking my hand and kissing the back.

'Are you?' I asked, trying not to be swept away by his charm.

'Am I what?' he asked, still holding on to my hand.

'James Bond?'

He looked me in the eye. 'If that's who you want me to be.'

'Oh please,' I said, causing us both to laugh at his obvious line. 'Who are you really?'

'Can we do that later?' he said, with a sudden serious tone.

It took every ounce of resolve I had, but I managed a weak, unconvincing counter-response. 'I don't think so.'

He kissed my hand again. 'You're the detective, you tell me who I am.'

I narrowed my eyes and looked closely at him as if trying to get clues from his face. He set his face in a confident almost-smile that tensed his jaw muscles. The look sent a shot of recklessness to my core that mingled with the wine and resulted in an absolute abandon of concern as to who he was. I stopped caring. For a night, I didn't want to care. We called for a car and ended up back in my room where there were no more questions or paranoia — just Bond and one of his girls.

6

I woke up early and called Kirk. I was under no obligation to check in with him, but knew he'd be getting worried. He'd texted me a couple of times since I'd arrived and I'd ignored them. But if I didn't respond soon he'd start sending people to find me and I didn't need that headache.

'Well, well, well, if it isn't my long lost ex-wife. Where've you been hiding yourself, Irish?'

'Oh, just here and there.'

'Getting rest?'

I looked over at Martin sleeping soundly in my bed. 'Yes sir, just like the doctor prescribed.'

'Seriously, where are you?'

'That's for me to know.'

'Ah, well, as long as you're still in the U.S. on safe ground, I don't care.'

I didn't feel badly for this particular misunderstanding. It was his assumption that I was still in the States, not my lie. 'I'm safe and sound.'

'Why are you whispering?'

'Again, that's for me to know.'

'Irish, are you trying to make me jealous?'

'Is it working?'

'Nah, if you are with someone, and he's a good guy, I'd say you deserve it. You should be enjoying yourself.'

'I don't know Kirk, I feel guilty.'

'I don't exactly enjoy the thought of you with another man, but we are divorced sweetheart, you have every right.'

I couldn't help but laugh out loud and fought to stifle my laughter when I saw Martin stir. 'Not because of you, you idiot! I feel guilty because I'm in no place to start a romance with anyone. I just got carried away in the moment. I should be focused on Danny and the fact that I have an undetermined amount of time to live.'

'First of all you should not be focused on Danny. Let. It. Go. Secondly, we all have an undetermined amount of time to live. Maybe the fact that you're giving in to a bit of unplanned fun should be an indication that you need this break.'

Martin was stirring again.

'I'd better go.'

'Wait, Irish, just another second.'

'Ahh, are you missing me Kirk, trying to keep me on line?' As I said it a realization struck me. 'Kirk! Are you tracing this call?'

'No, I just . . . '

I didn't stick around to find out what his defense was going to be. I hung up and crawled back into bed with Martin. He was awake and watching me on the phone.

'Should I be jealous?' he asked in a groggy, British-accented, morning voice.

I tucked up next to him and laid my head on his chest. 'That's the second time this morning a man has asked me that.'

He kissed the top of my head. And we let the question hang in the air without a response.

'Right here,' he said.

'Right here what?'

'My favorite place to wake up.'

I didn't respond. I stayed in his arms and mulled over Kirk's statement. Perhaps subconsciously my mind and body were telling me to give myself a break. I couldn't explain how the same woman who got off the plane yesterday, determined to take out anyone who got in her way, was now lounging in bed with a stranger. I was beginning to think that I didn't want to know who he was. What difference would it make? By the end of the morning he'd be off to his life in London, or back to his Grand-mère's, or to wherever his real life takes him.

★ ★ ★

We ordered room service and ate on the balcony in our white hotel robes.

'So where to now, Mr. Bond?'

'I haven't a single plan for the day.'

'Really? Don't you have a job?'

'Yes,' he said with a half smile, 'of course. Did you think you'd taken up with a sponger? Although, I have to say, your suite is quite a bit nicer than mine.'

'Where are you staying?'

'Grand-mère's,' he said suppressing a smile, fully aware of the humor in the juxtaposition of Granny's room to my suite. I doubted the truth in it, but couldn't help but laugh at the thought of him tucked under an ancient patchwork quilt.

'So if you have a job, when do you need to get back to it?'

'Whenever they call. I'm a consultant.'

'Oh I see, consultant, the vaguest of job titles.'

'It is rather vague, isn't it? But I truly don't intend it to be. It just happens to be what I do. Companies hire me for my vast amount of knowledge and expertise,' he said nonchalantly while spreading jam on his toast.

I began to probe. 'Your vast amount of knowledge in what area?'

He held up the toast, offering me a bite. I leaned in and bit the corner.

'I see your intelligence-gathering techniques rising to the surface, perhaps *you* should be Bond in our little tale.'

'Perhaps you should just answer the question.' I said it with a smile but it wasn't my intel-gathering rising to the surface, it was my paranoia.

He wasn't rattled in the slightest. He was enjoying our foreplay, which could mean he really was a trained spy — good under pressure, or just a consultant, playing spy meets mysterious woman. 'I like this side of you,' he said casually and offering me another bite of his toast. 'Computers. Not very sexy I'm afraid. I think I rather like you envisioning me as a spy instead.'

I could handle a computer consultant. I hoped he was telling the truth. I wanted it to be the truth. It would be a whole lot less messy.

'What about you? If you're not here on vacation what are you doing here, in the beautiful French Riviera?' He poured milk into his tea not expecting to hear anything unusual in my response.

'I'm looking for someone.' It came out before I knew it. I figured there wasn't much to lose. He looked up from his tea, but didn't say anything, expecting me to continue. *Maybe he can help*, I thought. It was wishful thinking. I felt like a little girl with a puppy, I wanted to keep him. 'My brother, Danny.'

'I don't understand. He's missing?'

'Yes. It's a long story; one that you really don't want the burden of knowing, but as it stands now, he's missing and I need to find him.'

'My God, that's terrible.'

'It is.'

'Can I help?'

'I don't think so. Computer consultants aren't typically the guys called for this sort of trouble. But if my computer breaks you'll be the first one I phone.'

His expression changed. I realized I had bruised his ego, or at least that's what I assumed. 'I'm sorry,' I said, 'I have a tendency to get sarcastic when I'm stressed.'

He reached for my hand and gave it a gentle squeeze. 'You don't need to apologize. You're right, I doubt I'd be able to offer much assistance, but I am great at moral support.'

His cell phone rang, punctuating the moment with a heavy period. He ran into the suite to answer it, leaving me on the balcony to look out onto the Mediterranean Sea and wonder if I'd made a mistake.

7

Martin's conversation was short, almost too short to even qualify as a conversation. I didn't hear him say a single word, not even hello. He returned with a new mood that, since I'd just met him, I couldn't identify. It's one of the difficulties in new relationships, not that this could qualify as a relationship just yet, but the man who got up from the table was not the same one who returned.

During our marriage, and in our current status as friendly exes, Kirk and I have gotten uncannily adept at reading the subtle changes in one another's moods. Each of us can identify a tired sigh from a stressed-out sigh from a guilty sigh. It reminds me of what mothers say about identifying their child's needs based solely on the tone of the child's cry. But when Martin returned, kissed my cheek and sat down, he didn't sigh; he didn't mention the call, he didn't smile, or seem tense, attentive or inattentive. He seemed — emotionless.

'Everything okay?'

'Yes, yes, just work. I have a job coming.'

'Oh,' I said, waiting for him to continue but he didn't. I didn't want to get too curious, but I couldn't figure out what could have changed in the space of one fifteen-second, phone call. 'Does that mean you need to be back in London today?'

'Not sure yet. I have to wait for more information,' he said, spooning strawberries into a dish but not offering any more details.

'Oookay then. How about the berries, delicious huh?'

'Yes, wonderful,' he responded, completely missing, or completely ignoring my sarcasm. Then without notice he completely returned to earth and brought the warmth back to his voice.

'Tell me Jackie,' he said, holding the small white dish, brimming with red berries, 'how do we find your brother? Where do we start?'

After a failed marriage you'd think I'd be smart enough to know when not to press a man. But I'm afraid I'm a slow learner when it comes to what makes a relationship work. He was changing the subject. 'That was an abrupt left, are you keeping secrets from me already?' He laughed so warmly that I couldn't believe a moment of frigid waters had ever flowed between us.

'I think I should be asking you that question, you're the one who snuck out of my bed this morning to call another man.' He was teasing, and I was enjoying the humor in his voice, but I knew there was a hint of seriousness to the statement. I decided not to let him off the hook; I decided to bite instead.

'My bed. I snuck out of my bed, to call another man.'

'Yes, defeated on a technicality I suppose.' He got up and took the plates into the suite's kitchen. I followed. I pushed myself up onto the counter. He came and stood in front of me, putting his hands on my hips.

'I'm serious Jackie, I want to help find

your brother in whatever way I can. I know you said I wouldn't want the burden of knowing, but if it's burdening you wouldn't it be nice to lighten the load? I can navigate the whole French Riviera like the back of my hand and I know quite a few people. Maybe I can make some calls.'

'Why? Why would you want to help me? You've just met me.'

'I haven't the slightest idea.' He wrapped his arms around my waist and laid his head on my chest. 'It would be nice to have a greater purpose I suppose, chase something besides the wind.'

I ran my hands through his hair. *What am I doing*, I thought. *Who is this man?*

He pulled away and interrupted my thoughts. 'I'm going to shower,' he said, 'do you mind if I borrow your shampoo? It's quite lovely how you've managed to have it bottled and labeled with those cute little monograms.' He was referring to the fact that the shampoo, along with the bed, was not actually mine. His wittiness had returned.

'Very funny,' I conceded with a little

laugh. 'Touché. By all means, have at it. Maybe all those little secrets you're keeping from me will wash off.'

He kissed me sweetly, lifted me off the counter and held me off the ground in his arms. He slowly lowered me to the floor and whispered in my ear. 'No secrets Jackie,' he said, then kissed my cheek and walked off into the bathroom.

'Not yet maybe.' The words, spoken in a breathy whisper, too quiet for him to hear, trailed after him as he walked away. 'But they're coming, aren't they?'

I remembered seeing a self-defense expert on an episode of Oprah. He was a large, broad-shouldered man, with a thick mustache and a full head of thick, graying hair. He was a former cop who I could easily picture in the uniform. He looked straight into the camera with intensity in his eyes and said: 'If you get the sense you're in the slightest bit of danger — get out!' He emphasized the statement by pointing his finger right at the lens. *No problem*, I had thought, looking right back at him through the screen, *I'm no victim.*

Besides trying to keep myself from snooping through Martin's bag as he showered, I replayed the cop's face in my mind, his finger pointing at me. I knew this was one of those moments he was talking about. I needed to tap into my instincts and listen. But my rebelliousness out-muscled my paranoia. I knew Martin wasn't telling me everything. I wasn't completely unaware of the potential danger in my situation with him. I was making a conscious decision to enter into a potentially dangerous situation. *I can handle this*, I thought.

8

Martin returned from the shower and became focused on getting the day started. He was less playful, more reserved. He moved about the suite quietly, fastening his watch, intensely looking through his bag and checking his phone. He came back from the shower as the person I'd envisioned him to be when I first saw him in the airport — a sighting I'd not yet confessed.

I tend to create personalities and characteristics for people that catch my attention. I've been known to create entire lives for the strangers I see on a regular basis. I'm sure the people I see at the gym every day, but never speak to, would be fascinated by the lives they live in my mind. I've practically scandalized the poor guy who stands in line with me at Starbucks every day. For all I know he's a perfectly wonderful man, but in my thought life, he's not to be trusted. I see it as people-watching, but taken one step further. It also makes me wonder what stories people have come up with about me. I wonder if any of them have created a story even half as interesting as the truth — a dying woman chasing her delinquent brother across the world. Oh, the drama.

After Martin collected himself he began quizzing me about Danny. His list of questions seemed random, a grasping at straws. He wanted to know things like Danny's favorite celebrities or foods or any of our favorite cousins or pets from childhood — potential passwords. His plan, he said, was to hack into his online accounts or see if he had any active social media profiles. We sat at the glass kitchen table.

'What about his phone carrier, I could probably hack into his phone records.'

I was amused at the thought of Martin sitting at a computer hacking. I picture computer hackers all wearing hoodies and drinking caffeine-fueled energy drinks while speed metal pumps in the background. 'You really are a computer geek aren't you?'

'I do try.'

'Well, as far as I know he's been using pre-paid phones. He's been on the run for quite a while and is getting good at not being found. But it was a good thought.'

Undeterred he continued. 'Social media? A lot of people who want access to social media but don't want people to find them will come up with fake names. The names are usually not impossible to guess if you know the person well enough.'

'I'm sure he's not trolling Facebook while on the run from the Mob and Interpol and most State and local law enforcements.'

He didn't seem surprised or shocked. He just frowned. 'No, I suppose not. I didn't realize when you said he was in trouble that you meant it quite so literally.'

'Well, yeah, as I said, it's a bit of burdensome information.'

'Which Mob?'

I was surprised by his question. Most

people, or maybe just most Americans, when hearing the word Mob, immediately think *The Sopranos* — dark-haired men, gold pinky rings, shirts opened one button too far, loveable pasta-eating tough guys. Not very many people even think about other forms of organized crime.

'Russian.'

He let a little bit of alarm spread across his face. 'Jackie, that's more than a little bit of trouble. The Russian Mafia is infamous for their ruthlessness.'

'Nah, Kaslov? He's a kitten. His henchmen treated me like a princess.'

'Please tell me you're joking. You didn't actually confront them?'

'Well, not exactly.'

'What does that mean?'

'Well, I didn't intentionally go out of my way to confront them, but I've found it a little difficult to stay out of their way.' He just stared at me for a few seconds, collecting his thoughts I assumed. 'Look Martin, it's really nice of you to want to help me, but you really don't want to get involved. I'm basically a stranger. You don't need to feel guilty for just walking away.'

He took my hand and squeezed it tightly. 'I'm not the type. I don't walk away.'

'But we're not . . . '

He interrupted me. 'I don't just walk away.'

* * *

We hired a driver to get us back to our cars. Martin arranged to have my rental returned to the hotel, and said we could take his car to hunt for Danny. He said he knew a few people who might be able to help. I was dubious but didn't want him to know that.

When we arrived at the restaurant, Martin let me into his car then disappeared inside the restaurant. When he returned he was putting a manila envelope into the messenger bag slung over his shoulder. I didn't ask about it, it was none of my business, but I was more than curious. I was silently willing him to divulge but he didn't.

'Where are we going?' I asked while he punched some numbers into what seemed like a computer in the center console. He stuck a device in his ear, appeared to be listening to something. I looked around his car and realized it could double for a computer superstore.

'So this is quite a rental you've got here.'

He flashed a mischievous grin. 'I like gadgets. It's one of the perks of being a, what was it you called me, a computer geek?'

I looked around the car. 'Um, this is a bit more than your average computer geek. You could run mission control for Batman in this thing. I know you flew here, so how did you get your car here?'

He smiled and spun his head in my direction. 'I didn't think you realized.'

'What, that we crossed paths in the airport? I've been wondering this whole time if *you* realized it.'

'I notice almost everything,' he said, 'but I've been wondering the same about you. You didn't mention it.'

'Neither did you.'

He conceded with a slight nod of his head.

Since the conversation had been started, I decided to pry a little. 'So, how often do you go to church? Is it just an airport habit or do you attend regularly?'

He seemed to get uncomfortable.

'I'm sorry, that is absolutely none of my business.'

'No no, it's fine. I just . . . it's hard to explain.'

'You really don't need to, it's private. I get it.' I reached out and gently touched his arm. I wanted to reassure him I wasn't offended.

He looked over at me and in an instant his eyes seemed to flash a series of emotions, pain, confusion, comfort. I realized his eyes were reflecting the inventory of thoughts his mind was processing. He whipped his head back around, punched a few more numbers in the computer, reached under his seat — for what I don't know, he seemed to be just occupying his hands, steadying himself, regaining control. While he did so he spoke. 'Sometimes, I just need to know there's something in control of this madness.'

I thought back to the passage in Ecclesiastes that the Bible had been turned to in the airport prayer room. It said something about the futility of this life, a chasing after the wind. I wondered what demons he was fleeing.

'I get that.'

Martin didn't register my reply. He was looking in the review mirror. 'Buckle up,' he said, in an eerily calm, but darkly intense voice. I looked in the review mirror and saw a large grey SUV flying toward us. Before I could even turn my head back around, Martin was flying down the street in reverse toward the car. 'Buckle up now!' he shouted.

I did as I was told. 'Who is that?' I screamed. 'I was about to ask you the same thing,' he said, as we were still driving in reverse toward the car. As we drove towards them bullets started flying. 'Get down!' he yelled. I could hear bullets ricochet off the sides of the stone walls.

'What are you doing, are you crazy, you're going to crash into them.'

'Just hold on!'

Every muscle in my body tensed as I braced myself for impact. But as we came within inches of the SUV, Martin swerved and then it went past us firing bullets. We got to the street and Martin threw the car into Drive. Going faster than any car should be able to go, we fled the cobblestone alley with its charming brick archways and sweet little restaurant.

9

'What was that?'

'Sorry, you okay?' He barely glanced in my direction as he responded. His eyes were periodically scanning the rearview mirror as he continued speeding down the streets I wasn't familiar with. He didn't appear to be the slightest bit rattled. He was taking corners like a stunt driver, with the kind of accuracy that takes training. 'Take the battery out of your mobile,' he said.

'What? Why?'

'Just do it!' He threw his at me. 'Mine too.'

I followed orders like a good soldier, and hoped I'd gotten mixed up with the right side of this war. I held on to the sides of my seat and clenched my jaw. He turned another corner that led to another small alley. He slid the car into a small alcove that looked like it had been designed to receive deliveries.

I desperately wanted to know what was happening, but quickly realized my safety seemed to depend on his ability to focus, so decided to avoid nagging him until we were safe.

From our position we could see the street. Martin didn't say a word. All I could hear was the inconsistent pattern of my own breath. If Martin's breath was shaky, he hid it well.

Just as I was beginning to get restless and close to asking him how long we intended to sit there, the gray SUV flew by down the street we'd come from.

'Let's go. Hang on.' He sped out of our hiding space and took off down the alley. He didn't say where we were going, or who was chasing us, or what kind of danger we'd just entered. He just drove in silence. I love a strong silent type but after a near-death experience, I kind of like answers.

'So what course during your stint in computer tech. school did you have to take to learn to drive like that?'

'I need to think,' he said. It was a polite way of saying please shut up.

I'm not used to being sidelined. But I realized I needed to let him do whatever thinking he needed to do so we could get out of this situation alive. I looked out the window to get my bearings but it was a hopeless effort. He was driving so fast I couldn't make out street signs. I didn't even know what city we were in and then, after several quick turns, we weren't in the city at all anymore. Suddenly, there was nothing but farmland all around us. Little provincial farmhouses dotted the landscape. In all the times I'd been to the South of France as a vacationer, I'd never ventured away from the exclusive exorbitance of its resorts and luxurious seaside towns.

Martin continued to drive quickly but with less intensity. I'd noticed he'd shut down the computer. No cell phones, no computers. I realized he was eliminating any possibility of our location being traced. We turned off the road and headed down a stretch of dirt that couldn't be considered a road as much as a trail. A cloud of dirt followed. I thought of Kirk and any one of his luxury cars that he babied and pampered, refusing to drive through a construction area for fear of loose stones. Apparently Martin wasn't as concerned.

Suddenly he slowed and turned down another trail that led to a farmhouse. Behind the house was a small shed that looked just large enough for a small tractor and supplies. We drove into the shed and as we did the doors slammed shut behind us.

'Get out.' There was authority in his voice but his demeanor was calm. And as I got out of the car I realized I wasn't as rattled as I should have been. *I'm actually getting used to this sort of thing*, I thought. Being chased by people who want to get me out of their way had become part of my routine. It was nice to have someone with me who could handle himself and who didn't seem to want to kill me, not yet anyway.

I got out of the car and waited for further instruction. I was completely under his direction and on a need-to-know basis and I didn't like it. I wanted to be in control of the situation. But I wasn't sure whom I was dealing with. I needed to play it safe in order to get whatever information I could. He slung his bag over his shoulder, took my hand, and led me to the back of the shed. 'Come on.'

He pushed aside some paint cans and an old blanket on the floor to reveal a small trap door. He lifted it to reveal a small metal ladder. 'Go ahead.' It was a directive but his voice didn't imply that I didn't have a choice. I didn't feel like I was his prisoner. I hesitated but I followed the order. I wasn't sure what was happening but in that moment I felt like he was my best shot at surviving whatever it was we'd gotten ourselves into.

He saw my concern. 'It's okay, I'll be right behind you.' He said this as if it was supposed to be comforting.

I gave him a look that implied I wasn't so sure I wanted him right behind me. 'No offense, but I'm not confident that that's a good thing.'

He laughed as if it suddenly occurred to him that what we'd just experienced might cause me to question his standing.

He put his hand on my waist and pulled me to him. I had no reason to feel safe or comforted, but I did. 'You're safe here. You're safe with me, I promise.' He kissed me lightly on the mouth, took my hand and directed me to the ladder.

'Yeah,' I said, as I obediently headed for the ladder. 'You, the one with no secrets.'

I made my way down and heard Martin close the trap door behind him. I reached the bottom and stood in a completely darkened space. I made room for Martin, who came down right behind me, but just slightly. I was afraid to move around. I couldn't see anything. There was absolutely no light coming into the underground space.

'Don't move. The lights will come on in a moment. They're set on a timer.' As soon as he finished the sentence the lights came on to reveal the last thing I had ever expected.

'What is this place?'

'My office.'

'This isn't an office, this is . . . this is . . . I don't even know what this is.'

It was unlike anything I'd ever seen. It wasn't a huge room, maybe the size of a master bedroom in a mid-sized home. One wall was lined with a steel cage that contained an armory of weapons — handguns, rifles, missile launchers, bulletproof vests. This guy was either some sort of operative or a seriously delusional doomsday stockpiler. There was a state of the art computer system against the wall opposite the armory and a simple metal desk with additional computers, monitors and wires draping down the backside. Martin sat down and started clicking away. The computers on the table fired up. He seemed to be typing in code and I couldn't understand a word of it. Then, as if suddenly remembering I was just standing, shocked, in the middle of the room he turned to me. He took hold of both my arms. 'I'll explain, just sit down for a moment,' he said gently, directing me to a steel chair next to the table.

While he tapped away I thought about how I ended up in an underground cave. I thought about Danny running around like a scared rat up above. I thought about Kirk and realized he couldn't help me.

I didn't have any proof, but I was fairly certain he'd been responsible for getting me out of sticky situations just like this one, working out deals with the Feds, calling off Kaslov's thugs, tracing my phones and credit cards, paying rental car agents to attach GPSs trackers on my car, whatever he needed to do to keep me safe. But now, right now, he couldn't come to my rescue. My phone was off, my whereabouts unknown. I'd entered the country under a fake name. If Kirk had been the one helping me from behind the scenes I'd be out of luck this time. He wouldn't be able to find me. My safety, my mission was now in the hands of Martin, a man I didn't know if I could trust — a man that could kill me with any number of weapons that were less than five feet from me.

'Start talking,' I said. There was no emotion in my voice. I wasn't pleading, whining, tender, or indignant. I was composed and in control. I needed answers. I wasn't about to sit there like a helpless wreck.

He stopped and just rested his hands on the edge of the table. He hung his head and took a deep breath. He looked at me from the corner of his eye, shook his head and released his breath in an exasperated sigh. 'Okay.'

10

Martin ran his hands through his hair and I noticed a scar on his forehead that I hadn't noticed before. Yesterday I would have guessed it was from a childhood bike accident, or maybe a tree-climbing incident. Now I assumed some type of hand-to-hand combat fight. It's amazing how one high-speed chase and a cache of weapons can change your perspective.

He pulled up a chair and faced me. 'What do you know?'

'No, no, no, I'm not going first. You spill it.'

'I'm not sure you want to know what's going on.'

'Believe me Martin, I'm not new to this. Are you supposed to kill me?'

His eyes flew open. 'What? No! Jackie, do you really think . . . ' I didn't give him a chance to finish his thought. I just shot him a look that said, are you kidding me, and gestured to the weapon-lined wall.

He looked over at them, as if he hadn't thought about what that might look like. He looked back at me, and as if getting it, responded. 'No, I've not been instructed to kill you.'

'Well that's a relief. Who was that trying to kill us?'

'I was hoping you'd know. To be honest, I was a little concerned by the fact that you didn't seem all that surprised that people were chasing us down an alley firing bullets.'

'Yeah, well, I've gotten used to a lot of drama in my life lately. You really don't know who they are?'

'I have no idea. As I said I was hoping you'd know.'

'If they were after me, they could've been any number of people.'

'Brilliant. That goes for me as well.' He paused for a moment and steadied himself as if he was about to tell me something that might shock me. 'Jackie, I'm not a computer consultant.'

'No, really? You're kidding?' His sincerity was actually endearing and perhaps a little insulting at the same time. How stupid did he think I was?

'Yes, well, I guess that's obvious now, isn't it?' he said, with a slightly self-chastising smile.

'Uh yeah, a little bit.'

'I'm British Secret Intelligence.'

'MI6?'

'Oh, I see you've heard of us.'

'Ha, yeah, as I've said, I'm not new to this.' He smiled and we both relaxed a bit.

I had been pretty confident that he wasn't with Kaslov and felt mildly better that he was MI6 but not a lot. I'm not high on anyone's list right now. 'So how did you know I was here?'

He looked at me with a confused squint of his eye. 'I didn't. I don't have any directive pertaining to you.'

'What's in that envelope you've been carrying around? The job you received?'

'I don't know yet.'

'I don't understand. Haven't you been tailing me?'

He shook his head. 'No. I noticed you in the airport because you're a beautiful woman who wanted to be noticed. Not because I had orders to find you. I didn't know you were trying to draw out leads to Danny. I didn't know anything about Danny.'

I thought back to the airport. He was right, I'd strutted through there hoping to get noticed and gather intel. 'So are you telling me our meeting was a coincidence? Forgive me for finding that hard to believe.'

'I don't believe in coincidences either, but this was not by design, not mine anyway. However . . . '

'Here we go, the however.' My tone was indicating my impatience.

'You asked about the envelope, my orders.' His voice was tender.

'Yep.' My voice was edgy and defensive.

He reached out and put a hand on my leg and tilted my head up so he could look me in the eye. 'I don't believe in coincidences,' he repeated as if trying to get me to understand the deeper meaning in what he was saying.

'I'm not following,' I said, probing for more information. He was being as vague as possible, a good quality for a spy.

'Look, the agency knows I'm here.

They made the arrangements. There are no coincidences. Whatever is in that envelope could link us through professional means.'

'Meaning?'

'That envelope could very easily contain orders for me to eliminate you, Danny, whoever is chasing you, whoever you were on the phone with this morning, I don't know. But I don't think our paths have crossed by accident.'

'But there's no way that anyone could have planned for us to find each other at the festival.' As I said it, I thought back to the shuttle driver from the airport, telling me all about the Mimosa festival, the Russian couple arguing. Who knows if either encounter was planned, but it made me more aware of the power of suggestion.

'Look,' he said, 'I've been doing this a long time. The world and the people who seem to run it are a tightly linked group. They have a way of moving the chess pieces without anyone even noticing. If we'd not found each other there, it would have happened somewhere else.'

I hated the comparison to chess pieces, but as much as I hated it I couldn't deny it. I thought about Kirk and how he managed to bring people in and out of my path without me realizing, or at least I assumed it was him. If he could do it, so could the British Secret Service, Kaslov, Interpol, anyone with enough power. Pawns, I thought, how cliché.

'But so what, why not just give you orders to find me?'

'I don't know. My guess is if you're as seasoned as you say you are they figured you'd be suspicious of me.'

'I was.'

'I know.'

'So what now?' I asked.

'I don't know yet. I'm not even sure my suspicions are correct. I was at that festival to track a Russian male linked to crimes against the British government. While I was there, they called off the hit. The guy was already out of France. Then I met you. As far as I'm concerned, as of right now we're still a man and a woman who met on vacation in the French Riviera.'

'That's lovely, except you're leaving out the part about us hiding in your secret bunker after having been chased by someone shooting at us and a manila envelope that could contain your orders to kill me.'

'Yes, about that. I hope you don't take it personally.'

'Business is business.'

'That's the spirit.' He leaned in and tried to kiss me.

'You're kidding right? You can't possibly think I'm going to let you touch me when you could be holding my death warrant.'

'I suppose that does change things.'

'Maybe just a little.'

'Jackie, I'm not going to kill you, no matter what that order says.'

'Yeah, and that little old lady from the festival is your dear sweet Grand-mère.' I didn't let him try to deny it or cover it up. I didn't care if it was truth or fiction. Both of us were liars. I couldn't fault him. I wanted to get back to business. 'The Russian and his girl have left France already?'

'How did you know he was with a girl?'

'I saw them in the hotel lobby at breakfast yesterday. I followed them to Mandelieu-Napoule but never found them at the festival. I was hoping they'd lead me to Danny.'

'Instead they led you to me.'

'Yep.'

'Not quite the consolation you were hoping.'

'Why do you say that? A romantic holiday tryst with a man who might have orders to kill her is every girl's fantasy.'

'Okay, okay,' he said, pacing the room. 'Let's figure this out. Why would I have orders to kill you? Are you a threat to anyone?'

'As far as I know, I'm a bargaining chip. Everyone who is looking for Danny hopes they can follow me to him. I don't think anyone is trying to kill me specifically, but they're not all that concerned if I get caught in the crossfire either.'

'Who'd want to just de-rail your mission?'

'What do you mean, just de-rail?'

'Well, those guys who were shooting at us in the alley weren't trying to kill us. Or if they were, they were doing a bloody awful job of it. They certainly weren't professionals.'

I thought about what he was getting at. Who would want to scare me, but not hurt me — someone who wouldn't want me to find my brother, who wouldn't want me running around with a handsome Brit through the South of France. 'Kirk.'

'I'm sorry, who?' he asked.

'No one. Never mind, I can't prove it anyway.' I was hesitant to spill too much. I was furious with Kirk but didn't want to put him in harm's way. He must have gotten enough of our conversation to trace my call. I didn't know if Martin was trying to help or pump me for information and I didn't want to provide him with much. 'Well, it didn't work. I'm not scared.'

He stopped pacing for a moment and looked at me. 'Yes, I've noticed that. I've seen a lot of people in near-death situations, there's a degree of panic that distorts a person's face when they believe someone's trying to kill them. You didn't have that look.'

'Well, death is coming for all of us at some point, no sense in panicking about it.'

'That's a rather grim outlook.'

'Well, when you're dying it's nice to know you're not really alone in the matter.'

He froze. 'Come again?'

'Yeah, I know, it's a shock. Cancer. But I don't need your sympathy, or your comfort. Right now I'm fine and I just need to find my brother. All I need from you is your help.' He reached out for my hand and helped me up. He wrapped me in his arms. 'Ahh, how sweet,' I said, as he kissed the top of my head. 'An assassin with a soft spot.' I didn't bother to tell him that this particular scene actually is every girl's fantasy. Every girl wants to believe that she's the one able to bring warmth to the cold heart of a dangerous man.

He laughed and released me just enough to look me in the eye. 'I'm an assassin, Jackie, not a sociopath. Killers have feelings too.'

I leaned my head into his chest and felt relieved by his humor. 'A modern day prince charming.'

11

We'd been down in the bunker for at least an hour. Martin gathered intel from a secure line, former assets, known snitches, anyone trying to fly under the radar that might lead us to Danny. The mood in the bunker seemed lighter now that some secrets had been revealed. But the manila envelope resting, unopened, on the cold metal table seemed to be doing its best to suck the nice clean air out of the room. My hunch was that it contained a hit order on my brother. It was probably filled with all the information we needed to get us directly to him. But if we opened it, it would also mean Martin would have to do his job.

'It's suffocating in here.'

'You get used to it.' Martin was working to collect some weapons and extra clips.

'Do you shoot?' He held up a black

handgun and offered it to me. I didn't take it.

'I loathe guns.'

'You get used to that too.'

'Never.'

He looked down at the gun in his hand and a shadow of sadness fell on his face. 'Yes, perhaps not.'

I realized that the fact that he was even offering me a gun meant that a degree of trust had been established. It made me nervous. I'd gotten used to eliminating the 'T' word from my vocabulary, and was certain that up to this point in his career, Martin wasn't in the habit of trusting anyone either. We were both on new ground.

He was still looking at the gun in his hand. 'Martin?'

He looked at me and again tried to hand the gun to me. 'Take it.' The sadness was still on his face.

'I wouldn't know what to do with it.'

'I'm going to teach you. Let's go.' He turned to head up the ladder.

I looked down at the gun in my hand. It was disgusting. I was not in denial about the new version of my life or the darkness that filled my new world. The safe, reliable, tidy film that used to cover my world had been permanently peeled back to reveal pain, death, and seediness. But in that moment, gripping that cold steel, it was as though I was holding all that darkness in my hand, my fingers straining against its weight.

He packed up the rest of his things and headed back up the ladder. I watched him climb. 'Hey, Martin,' I shouted up to him. He paused and looked down at me. 'How do you know I won't just shoot you and run?'

He climbed back down the ladder. Stood confidently in front of me and looked me in the eye. He reached a hand behind my head and brought my lips to his. He kissed me as if he'd known my lips all his life. I let the darkness that was weighing me down seep out of my body. He pulled away and looked me in the eye again.

'Jackie,' he whispered. 'It's not loaded.' He smiled and climbed back up the ladder.

I laughed and followed him up. 'Yeah, well, you're lucky.'

'Luck is for the fool,' he said.

★   ★   ★

We walked for at least a mile to fields dotted with old trees. We were in the middle of nowhere. He set up targets and taught me how to load and shoot the Glock .45. He showed me how to holster it, draw, point and fire. I've seen scenes like this in the movies — handsome guy teaching helpless girl to fire a gun, standing behind her, whispering in her ear. It's a romantic setup. This wasn't the way it felt. The mood was somber, and the reality of what we were doing was never more than a thought away. I was sick to my stomach the whole time. But I forced my nerves to be still. Once he was sure I could handle myself if absolutely necessary we packed up and headed to the car. I just prayed it wouldn't be necessary.

As we walked back through the field toward the shed, we were quiet, but the sound of gunfire was still ringing in my head. As horrible as it was to know that there was a gun strapped to my body, there was also a sense of power that came with it. I liked it, and that frightened me. I could imagine pulling the trigger and killing Kaslov and his thugs. Who was I becoming?

'Is this how assassins are born, Martin?'

'I don't think you have to worry about that just yet.'

'It changes you, permanently, doesn't it?' It's easy to imagine taking the life of someone you hate, but living with the reality of it is something entirely different.

He didn't look at me, he just answered, 'If there's goodness in you, it changes you forever.'

'Why do you do it?'

'It's my job.'

'Why.'

'I don't know.'

'Don't you ask?'

He stopped me. 'Look Jackie, it's not that simple. I wake up every day and wonder why I live like this, trying to convince myself that I'm doing good, that I'm only killing people who deserve to die — the greater good and all that bloody nonsense. It doesn't do me any good to ask questions that will never be answered. I get a job, I do the job. That's it, that's the end of it.'

'But it's not the end of it, is it? That verse you were reading in the prayer room. Something about the work done being grievous. This grieves you? You're not a killer.'

'I am, by very definition, a killer.'

The words hung between us and an aching grew in my heart. He was a killer. He had a job to do.

We remained quiet as we walked back through the field. As we approached the shed he stopped.

'Jackie, I'm going to have to pop back on the grid. If I don't they'll just send another agent to do the job that was meant for me and they'll find me and bring me in.'

'What does that mean? What are you saying?'

'I'm going to have to find out what my

assignment is and respond.'

'Then what?'

'I don't know. That's why I wanted to be sure you could protect yourself.'

'Against who?'

'I don't know.' He was getting frustrated and raising his voice.

'Martin, against who? You?'

'No, I already told you that I wouldn't kill you even if the order was for you. But I think we both know it's not for you, it's for Danny. There's chatter all over the place about him. Everyone wants him and I'm in proximity. I know that envelope contains his dossier and so do you.'

His acknowledgement silenced me. I knew he was right. It would be naïve to think Martin and I could fly under the radar, find Danny and have our little reunion, then return to the realities of life. He wasn't a P.I.; he was a trained assassin.

We entered the shed and he laid his bag on the hood of the glossy black Bimmer. He lifted the envelope out of the bag and handed it to me.

'Go ahead.'

I opened it and pulled out a file containing several black and white photos of my brother, a list of aliases and known associates. There were a few pictures of me, a directive to acquire me as an asset, and a shoot to kill order for Danny. My heart sank as I handed it to him.

'Well, it looks like you're on target so far. You're very good at your job.'

He took the file. 'You're my asset.' He seemed relieved. 'This is a good thing.'

'How do they even know I'm here? I entered with a fake passport.'

'Face recognition software when you went through security at the airport. Your image alerted the agency.'

'Great, the face that launched a thousand ships.'

'Something like that, yes.'

'Now what?'

'Now I tell them that the asset is secure and willing.'

'Willing to . . . ?'

'Willing to cooperate. It also says I'm meant to keep you safe and alive. And then return you to American soil. Your safety is apparently a top priority. You must have some pretty powerful ties.'

I thought of Kirk and wondered if this was his doing. Martin continued to flip through the file. 'I'm not willing to cooperate.'

He didn't look up; he was studying the report. 'You don't have a choice.'

'Don't you dare. I'm not your asset. This is my mission. I will not be assisting you in the assassination of my brother.'

He didn't respond to my outburst. He took on the same persona he had when he'd received the phone call requiring him to come back to work. He just filed the dossier back in his bag and grabbed the extra ammunition he'd brought up from the bunker.

'Martin! Do you hear me?'

'Get in.' He appeared emotionless again but I could see restraint. He was holding back.

'I'm not getting in this car until I know what your plan is.'

'I don't know!' he shouted. 'I don't know what my plan is! You think I planned this? Any of it!' He put his head down and slammed his hands on the hood of the car, the sound echoing off the walls of the metal shed. We both just stared at each other. He lowered his voice but kept his eyes on mine. 'You need to trust me.'

I reined in my temper and matched his tone. 'Martin, you're insane if you think I'm going to follow you around while you gather information that will lead you to my brother.'

'Disaster. Utter disaster.' He was flustered. I could see him regretting his decision to buy me that glass of wine. I suspect at the time we both knew it was a bad idea, and yet a moment of indecision about the paths our lives had taken us on led us to want a moment of normalcy. We'd wanted to be two random travelers enjoying a romantic vacation fling. We wanted to leave behind the trained assassin and the dying woman desperate to find her delinquent brother. We were reckless. We were impulsive. We were stupid. And now we were stuck.

'I can't go with you unless you promise me you won't kill Danny.'

'How can I promise that? It's my job.'

'He's my brother.'

He came over to me and put a hand on my arm. 'Jackie, have you ever wondered why so many people want him dead? I know he's your brother but do you ever wonder if you're on the wrong side here?'

I stiffened against his touch. 'I know you need to convince yourself that the people you kill are evil villains, I know it's the only way for you to sleep at night, but you've got it wrong this time.' My voice was cold and strong. I needed to capitalize on his doubt. I wanted to take advantage of the mistake he made by getting emotionally involved. He was obviously struggling with the actions his occupation required him to take, and I pounced on his doubt. I didn't want him to escape the reality of what he was being asked to do. I didn't want him to disappear into an emotionless state so he could justify killing Danny if given the opportunity. It was emotional sabotage.

He was listening intently and I could see uncertainty in his eyes. I softened my voice. 'Danny is a mess. He's been strung out for so long he can't even begin to recognize a clear thought. He was in the wrong place at the wrong time and messed with the wrong people. He's running scared and making stupid decisions fueled by drugs and paranoia.' I paused, thinking about the day I'd finally caught up with him in New York. I was finally face to face with him as bullets flew by us. That horrible day in our hometown, the town of our childhood, he looked at me with sheer terror and venom. He thought I'd betrayed him. It made my heart ache for him and I desperately wanted to find him. I needed to make Martin understand. I looked at him with pleading in my eyes. 'He's all I have, Martin. In a lot of ways he's just a little boy who's struggling to cope with the death of our parents.' This revelation seemed to sting him. 'And now he's going to have to face the death of his sister.' I was laying it on thick, obnoxiously so, but it was my only shot at getting him to promise me he'd help me save Danny, not kill him. I'd even produce tears if I had to. I wasn't above playing the desperation card.

'Stop Jackie, just stop.'

'Please Martin.'

He pulled me to him and I let him wrap his arms around me. He kissed me with intensity and passion. He wanted to make it go away, for both of us. He pulled away and held my face in his hands. 'I will do everything I can to keep you both alive. Then I'll leave the agency. This will be my last job.'

'I'm sorry, Martin, I'm so sorry.'

'Don't be. I'm not. It's over. And, truthfully it doesn't have much to do with you. I simply can't do it anymore. I don't have it. Once you make room for your conscience, start questioning your actions, it's the end. There's no going back.'

12

The plan was to go back into town and find a drug pusher named Julien. Apparently my talking about Danny's drug issues sparked an idea for Martin. He said if Danny was looking for a fix, Julien would know about it. He said Julien had the market cornered with dealers all over the Riviera. I thought it was as good a place as any to start. I was sad to acknowledge that the best place to track Danny was through his drug contacts, but it was the truth.

We were driving along the coastline. I was almost able to believe nothing had happened, that all the secrets were still in the closet.

We drove in silence for a while but my thoughts were getting too loud and I needed to drown them out. 'How do you know Julien?'

A smile spread across his face. 'We were kids together.'

'You're not telling me that tale you spun about Grand-mère was actually true, and you actually spent summers here?' I could picture him playing in the surf, a tanned little boy chasing the waves long before the horrors of his adult life were even a glimmer of possibility. Again a smile warmed his face as if he could see my thoughts and himself in the surf as a child. It wasn't hard to see why I was so quick to fall for him.

'Do you want it to be?' He took his eyes off the road for a moment to meet my mine.

I turned my face away from his and looked out the window, relaxing against the headrest. 'Yes.'

'Then it's true.'

I let the lie warm my heart. He reached over, took my hand and brought it to his lips.

'One day we'll have to visit Grand-mère together,' I said.

He laughed and we exchanged a smile that acknowledged we were both in on the joke. 'Yes,' he said, 'I think she'd love that.'

I'd had enough reality to last me a lifetime. I wanted to live in the fantasy for a while longer.

'Is Julien someone we can trust?'

'One never knows.'

'Great, that's comforting.'

He nodded. 'At one time there was no one I could trust more. I'd have trusted him with my life, my wife, and my last pound.' Martin had a small smile on his face but it was far away, as though it was a memory that had put it there. 'Now I wouldn't trust him with much.'

We were both quiet for a moment and a solemn mood fell over both of us. I decided we needed a break in the tension. 'You have a wife?' I asked, grinning widely as if it had been the only detail I'd picked up on from his story. Thankfully he was quick-witted.

He looked at me, matching my grin. 'Oh, didn't I mention?'

We laughed. But the reality of the situation, and I don't mean just going to Julien's, I mean all of it, my cancer, his crisis of conscience, the disillusionment with this life we were both facing and the dark mood that accompanied it, filled the car within seconds. Reality is not a romantic getaway with an exciting stranger. It's messy, complicated and risky. It's no laughing matter.

13

Once we got into Cannes, where Julien was to be found, Martin drove with one eye on the rearview mirror. He tried to be subtle but I knew he was looking for company. I thought it was sweet he wanted to protect me from his concern; I didn't have the heart to give him all the details of what I've been through during my search for Danny, his worry was futile, I'd seen enough to have concern of my own.

It had been a long day and the end didn't seem to be in sight. The sun was hovering over the water as we made our way down the *Blvd de la Croisette*. The street was populated with lavish hotels and high-priced boutiques. Pansies and cyclamen filled flowerbeds along the sidewalk. Several lighted palm trees lined both sides of the street. Their iridescent glow filled the dusky sky with soft light. It wasn't difficult to imagine the street occupied by bronzed tourists during the summer months and celebrities during the annual film festival, the mood light and exhilarating. In my fantasy, Martin and I would sit at a cafe sipping wine and walk hand in hand into the shops.

I was woken from my daydream, of a life with Martin that would never exist, as we started driving through the *Quartier des Anglais*. Kirk and I had gone through once as tourists and half joked about buying one of the luxurious villas.

'Julien lives here?'

'Surprised?'

'Nothing surprises me anymore.'

'Julien comes from money and has made a lot more of his own providing whatever the wealthy residents, tourists, and celebrities need to have a good time.'

'Pathetic.'

'Yes.'

We pulled up to a gated residence that was designed to look like an Italian villa. We stopped at the speaker box and Martin said something in French that was apparently sufficient enough to cause the gates to glide open. There were guards patrolling the driveway.

We stopped the car next to a magnificent fountain. 'How quaint,' I said.

Martin didn't respond to my sarcasm. 'We'll have to leave the weapons in the car.' He spoke in a tone that said this was a business meeting.

I was grateful for the chance to get the gun off my body. We walked towards the double entry, front door. The strong hand-carved wood held delicate etched glass. The doors were so large they dwarfed the man who swung them open before we'd even made it up the steps. 'Martin!' A thin blond-haired man stood before us. His hair was cut short in the back but he had long loose bangs that hung just slightly over his left eye. He was wearing a navy blue track-suit and I laughed silently at his ode to David Beckham. *Europeans and their soccer*, I thought. Before we could make it up the steps one of the large guards approached us and ordered us to spread our legs with nothing more than a grunt and a wave of his hands toward our legs. I prepared myself for a pat-down. Martin rolled his eyes at Julien, who was now standing on the steps of the entryway.

'Forgive me, friends, business, you know.'

'Yes, just another day at the office,' Martin said, as the pat-down ended and we made our way up the steps. Martin and Julien embraced one another with a hearty laugh and a solid patting of one another's back and a kissing of one another's cheeks. They exchanged some pleasantries in French. From the outside it looked every bit like a couple of old friends reuniting after a long separation. No one would ever guess Martin was a spy slash assassin, I was a dying woman in search of her brother and Julien was a drug dealer. Looks can be deceiving.

Martin introduced me to Julien who took my hand in both of his and bowed his head slightly. He addressed me in heavily accented English. 'It's delightful to meet you.' Without releasing my hand he brought his head up to look me in the eye and held eye contact for longer than was necessary or comfortable. Martin stood between us putting one hand on my lower back and one on Julien's shoulder, squeezing it tightly. Julien turned to Martin and smiled arrogantly, understanding Martin's touch was meant as a signal to keep his hands and his leering eyes off.

'Come come,' Julien announced, with the arrogant smile still plastered on his face.

'Charming,' I whispered to Martin who took my hand with a gentle reassuring squeeze. We followed Julien through his mansion. It was designed with marble floors, marble columns, and fur rugs. *Nice*, I thought, *and not the least bit tacky* — yes, even my thoughts are sarcastic. As we walked through the house it was impossible not to notice the several large men, holding what appeared to be machine guns, strolling around the kitchen and balcony. There had been one stationed at the front door as well. I was amused by the degree of protection and wondered if Kirk wished he could protect me to this degree. I'd have my own Secret Service if it were left up to him.

Julien seated us in a large living room on a black leather sofa and sat opposite us on an identical sofa. A zebra print rug and a glass coffee table filled the space between us. There was a bar built into the wall just to my right, its glass shelves lined with beautiful crystal cocktail glasses. It was easy to imagine the parties that likely filled the house on a regular basis. From where I sat I could see the beautiful French doors leading to the wide balcony and a view of his lavish garden and swimming pool.

'So are you here to arrest me?' Julien asked, with a laugh that was several decibels higher than the joke warranted. Martin put on his cold steely demeanor and waited for Julien to settle down. '*Toujours tellement grave*,' Julien said, with a residual laugh. 'He's always been so serious,' he said, addressing me.

Martin seemed used to his teasing. 'Yes, well, some aspects of life require a certain degree of seriousness, don't they? By the way, Grand-mère sends her love.' This seemed to silence Julien immediately. He whipped his head in Martin's direction. The comment had momentarily stunned him. But he quickly regained his carefree, lighthearted posturing.

'Still trying to weasel your way into the family fortune Martin?' Julien was smiling but I could see there was seriousness to his statement. I was definitely intrigued by the background to their story and pleased that there seemed to be at least some truth to Martin's tale.

'You know I've never wanted any part of your inheritance, Jules.' Martin changed his tone, calling Julien by the nickname I could imagine he'd been using for Julien since childhood. I didn't know all the details but it was evident there was a far-reaching history between these two men. I sensed it pained Martin to see how Julien chose to spend his life. I wondered if it was why he decided to help me with Danny. He could relate.

Julien dismissed the uncomfortable topic with a wave of his hand. He clearly did not want to delve into the past. I was slightly disappointed. Although I wanted to get to information leading to the location of Danny, I was curious about the history.

'*Trieste*, no? So very sad. Poor Jules.' He spread his arms to indicate the luxury that surrounded him. 'It's no matter.'

Martin grew impatient. 'Listen Jules, we're looking for someone.'

'So?'

I decided it was time for me to step in. 'My brother.' Julien looked at me as an indication to continue. 'He's probably been to see one of your . . . um . . . associates. He . . . '

'Yes, yes,' Julien interrupted me, waving his hand again, indicating my explanation was unnecessary and boring him. 'The American running from everyone, yes, I know. He talks too much. He's going to get himself killed. He also owes me money. My men are looking for him as we speak.'

My heart was pounding hard enough for me to be aware of its presence in my chest. 'Where? Where is he? What does he owe you? I can pay it.' This seemed to get his attention. He smiled and stood up. He walked over to the bar and began to make himself a drink.

'Loyalty, *oui*. You remember, Martin?'

'*Oui*.' Martin said, playing Julien's childish game. But I was tired of Julien's antics.

'Get on with it, Jules.' I let his nickname roll off my tongue with acerbity, letting him know I was mocking him. I didn't have time for this little reunion. 'What does Danny owe you?'

'Oh, I see. So feisty,' he said with a laugh. He turned back toward us with two drinks. He handed me one and with his free hand tilted my chin so he could see my eyes. 'You always liked them like this, Martin. No? Feisty? Like Monique, eh, remember.' He had a laugh that made my stomach turn.

Martin stood up and for a minute I thought he might throw a punch. The two men were nose to nose. Immediately one of Julien's guards was at attention and there was a gun aimed at Martin's back. Julien raised a hand to call off the guard. The arrogant grin I'd quickly grown to despise appeared on Julien's face. Martin was unmoved by it.

107

'Sit down, Martin.' Julien's voice was playful. It was clear he didn't take anything seriously. 'She's clearly able to take care of herself. Aren't you Jacqueline?'

Julien turned away from Martin and walked lazily toward the sofa. His drink seemed to be barely hanging on to the tips of his fingers, threatening to drop at any moment. He exuded boredom. 'So, you want to find your brother? I don't think I can help you. He is of particular interest for me.'

'What interest could he possibly have for you? I can pay you whatever he owes.'

'I am not sure you can. Kaslov is quite generous and eager for your brother. Kaslov? You've heard of him, no?'

'You're a disgusting pig.'

Julien returned my remark with a hearty laugh.

'Let's go, Jackie,' Martin was standing, 'we're not going to get anywhere with him.'

'Oh, don't be that way, Martin, you just got here.' Julien was sitting with his legs crossed, sipping his drink.

'Jules.' Martin stopped and turned toward his old friend. 'You don't get it do you? Five minutes, it would take me five minutes to destroy you.'

Julien stood up. For the first time since we'd arrived his face was hard and the arrogant smile gone. 'Do not threaten me.'

'It's not a threat.'

I touched Martin's arm and looked at Julien. 'Just tell me what you want. What is Kaslov paying you?'

Julien brushed his shirt off as if the verbal warfare between him and Martin had soiled his clothes. 'It's not just about money, although the five million will be nice.'

'Yeah, I can see you need a few more animal prints in here. There's a few more levels of trashy you've yet to reach.' I didn't let him know that the price was enough to choke me. I couldn't believe Kaslov was willing to shell out five million for Danny's head.

Julien was not pleased by my remark about his taste. 'Martin, you need to teach this one manners.' He looked like he wanted to backhand me. I'd almost hoped he would, I wanted to see Martin take him out. But with all the guns in the room I knew it would be a stupid move on his part, and Martin wasn't stupid. I needed to watch my tongue and try to play nice.

The three of us stood there like school children just waiting for someone to make a move. It was Martin who finally broke the silence.

'What did he take? What is it that you can't possibly live without?'

Julien maintained eye contact with Martin. They were inches from one another. 'Not what, who,' Julien said, in a ragged, breathy whisper.

Idiot. Danny you are such an idiot. I rolled my eyes in disbelief.

Only my brother would run off with the girlfriend of the drug dealer he owes money to.

'What about you, Martin? What is your interest in our mutual friend?' Julien seemed to be challenging Martin. 'This is an official visit, no?' Martin didn't flinch. He just stared at Julien, daring him to keep it up. Julien looked at me. 'He's a killer, you know.' Julien was grinning. 'You better keep him happy. Do you keep him happy, Jacqueline?' He was eyeing me with a seductive gleam.

Before I could offer a tart response Martin's fist landed on Julien's jaw. Julien fell to the ground. Within seconds a gun was stuck in Martin's ribs. The gunman hesitated, waiting for his orders. It was a bad choice. He shouldn't have hesitated; before I knew what was happening Martin had grabbed the barrel of the gun, made a sudden twisting movement and suddenly had the gun pointed at Julien. 'Tell them to stand down, Julian!'

I was stunned into silence and immobility. Julien seemed just as stunned but within a moment began laughing. 'Just like when we were boys, no? Our days always ended in fights. Grand-mère would be so disappointed.' He began to get up. His laughter turned into a sigh. I thought he was actually losing his mind. He got to his feet and held his hand up to the gunmen to hold them off. Then he looked at Martin. 'Get out. Get out!'

Martin kept the gun and took my hand. But we never made it to the door. Before we could get there it flew open and an entourage of heavily-armed men stormed in. They didn't appear to notice or care about our presence. If they had, I'm sure they would have assumed I was a rich socialite looking for something to party with, visiting Julien for his professional services, Martin my protection.

'Where is he?' The leader of the troupe made it clear his visit wasn't a social one. His accent was unmistakably Russian. Kaslov had arrived — his presence anyway. He wouldn't actually show up to mess with Julien himself. There are people for that sort of dirty work.

'Yuri, so happy to see you, won't you come in.' Julien was annoyed. It was clear this was not how he'd envisioned his day would unfold.

The man Julien addressed as Yuri walked to the bar and began pouring himself a drink. He was obviously at home in the house. 'Come now, Julien, get to it, where's the American?'

'Funny you should ask. I was just

explaining my sad tale to my friends here.' Julien gestured toward us. I was grateful Martin still had the gun.

Yuri looked at us and shrugged. He didn't seem concerned by our presence. I was hoping Julien wouldn't announce my identity. I wanted to get out of that house without an altercation with Kaslov's men. But also I wanted to hang around long enough to find out Danny's location. 'Leave,' he said, in a bored tone.

Martin pulled me toward the door. I knew I should just turn and go, but I still didn't know where Danny was. I looked at Martin, trying to silently communicate that I needed to find some way to stay, when out of the corner of my eye I noticed one of Yuri's men and he noticed me at the same moment. We'd met before when bullets were flying overhead in New York. He knew who I was. 'Wait!' he yelled then walked over to Yuri. He whispered in Yuri's ear. I could feel the tension in Martin's body begin to rise.

'Jackie O'? Here, in person?' Yuri said to the room.

'Oh, so you've met?' Julien said smugly.

'What are you doing here?' Yuri asked me, looking straight into my eyes.

'I was just getting to that. My sad tale, remember?' Julien spoke for me.

Yuri was not amused by Julien and flashed him an annoyed sneer. Julien was unfazed by Yuri's disdain. 'You see, comrade, Jacqueline just offered to pay me for Monsieur O'Hara's location.'

'Is that right?' Yuri came over to me. 'You are the trouble-maker. My boss is not so happy with you.' Yuri turned to address Julien. 'I thought you said you had taken care of her?'

'I tried, but . . . '

'I tried, I tried . . . ' Yuri said, imitating Julien with a whining, complaining tone. As soon as he said it, I realized that the van shooting at us down the alleyway had been arranged by Julien. A 'private hire' Julien had called it. *Weasel*. I felt a twinge of guilt for blaming Kirk. But I also remembered what Martin had said. They were only trying to scare us. I understood that our danger was not with Julien or his men. Whatever history Martin and Julien had it ran deep and there was a degree of honor. Our only danger would come from Yuri and his men.

Yuri's comment filled me with childish satisfaction. He wanted me out of his way and I liked the fact that I'd become a nuisance to Kaslov and his men. I've always enjoyed being difficult to deal with. I held my tongue, still hoping to get information. Martin stood still and silent. I could feel his attentiveness. He was letting Yuri believe he had command of the room. As of that moment Yuri had no idea he wasn't just one of Julien's hired men keeping me in line.

Yuri turned away from me and started walking through the room, speaking loudly to no one in particular. 'So here we are. Everyone after the same piece of trash, like hungry birds.' He paused for dramatic effect. 'But where's the trash?' He was walking around the room speaking as if he was on a stage performing a monolog.

'He's run off with Michelle,' Julien finally said.

Yuri stopped, caught by Julien's admission. His back was to me so I couldn't see his expression but he started laughing loudly. He turned to face Julien, still grinning deviously. 'Michelle, your Michelle?' He started laughing again. 'I knew that girl was trouble, she was too smart for a junkie like you.' Julien hung his shoulders like a small child being shamed for his behavior. 'So tell me, where did the love birds run off to?'

Yes, yes, please get on with the only information that matters.

'Monaco,' Julien said, all the smug, irritating antics gone from his demeanor. I could see a look of confusion on the faces of his gunmen. They were watching their leader submit to this thug.

Mentally I was already in Monaco, elated I finally had a concrete location. But my elation was eliminated the minute Yuri spoke his next words. 'Let's go. And bring her with us.' One of Yuri's men walked over to me and grabbed my arm. Martin didn't move. I looked at him with fierceness, panic in my eyes. *He'd better be bluffing.*

116

Yuri walked toward the door confidently, knowing Julien had no fight in him or any reason to fight for me. He opened the door and was on the first step, thrilled about his prize. He wasn't expecting what happened next. My back was to the room; the jerk ordered to escort me out had already started pulling me toward the door. Suddenly shots rang through the room. The man, whose hand had been gripping me so tightly, had dropped to the floor, blood pouring from his skull.

In a matter of seconds, Martin was now the man gripping my arm and slipping me his keys. 'Get out the second you're able,' he whispered.

Yuri ran back in to find his man on the ground. Martin had his gun aimed at him and without hesitation fired. Yuri fell to the ground and Martin pushed me toward the door. The beautiful marble flooring that welcomed guests to *La Maison de Julien* was now covered in blood.

I ran for the car and was shaking in spite of my resolve to stay calm. The room had erupted in gunfire. Martin had guessed right. Yuri's crew would be more concerned with avenging Yuri's death than chasing after me and I got to the car safely. The last thing I heard before getting in the car was Julien's voice, 'Martin! No! No! No!' Julien's voice was filled with sorrow and panic. The unmistakable sound of grief over some-one you love. I turned to see Martin's body collapsed in the entryway. He'd stayed in the doorway to give me time to get away.

14

The sun had vanished completely and I was grateful for the darkness. I got into Martin's car and shut out the sound of the war that had erupted inside the house. I didn't waste time with tears. I started the engine and was down the driveway in an instant, slowed only by the mechanical gate. 'Come on, come on!' I shouted to no one. If Kaslov's men weren't right behind me, they would be soon, and I was certain that someone had to have called the police by now. It wasn't the sort of neighborhood that was used to hearing gunshots. I needed to get away from there as quickly as possible.

As I pulled away from Julien's I had only one thought in my mind: Monaco. It was all I could think about. If I allowed my thoughts to wander down any other trail they would take me to Martin and that was dangerous ground. It would be too easy to allow the guilt and sorrow to seep in. I knew Martin wouldn't want me to waste my time on either emotion. I knew what he'd say if he were here, that he wasn't new to this game and that his life was at risk long before he met me. Maybe, if I continued to remind myself of those facts, I just might make it through without feeling responsible. I knew the tears would come eventually. But not now, now I needed to assume Martin's professional demeanor, emotionless.

Martin had asked me if I ever thought about whether or not I was on the wrong side of this fight. Maybe Danny wasn't worth it. It was a question Kirk had posed on numerous occasions. I've never thought about it in terms of worth. To a lot of people Danny isn't worth much, but he's my brother. I can only consider it in terms of drive. I'm driven to reconcile with him before I die. I understand, or at least I think I do, what Martin was struggling with. He must have asked himself a million times whether he was on the right side. The right side — what's that? Are any of us?

I sped down the coast in Martin's

weapon-filled car. It was a race now — a race to Monaco, to Danny and to some woman named Michelle and hopefully to the end of this chase. Hopefully, the end would provide some sort of meaning, something to prove that it wasn't all just futility, a striving after the wind.

Part Two

1

That night I was standing at the roulette table in the *Salle Medicin*, one of five gambling rooms in the *Casino de Monte Carlo*, watching the guests entering and leaving. I was waiting for a specific man and finally, after about forty minutes and a string of losses, I saw him enter the old majestic casino and cross the crowded, brightly-lit room toward me. I lowered my head so he wouldn't notice me watching him, and placed my entire bet on twenty-one red.

He reached the roulette table and stood opposite me just as the wheel stopped spinning and the *croupier* called out: '*Vingt-et-un rouge!*'

I pumped my fist and yelled: 'Yes!'

Everyone around the table applauded, including the man. I smiled briefly at him and waited for the *croupier* to push my winnings to me. Then, dropping the chips into my purse, I ignored his invitation to the bettors to place their bets and walked over to the elegant bar. There were mirrors behind it and in them I could see the man watching me walk away. I added a provocative little swing to my hips, hoping this would invite him to follow me. It worked. Before I could give the bartender my order, the man had climbed onto the stool beside me.

To say he was hot is an understatement — but then what man isn't a knockout in a tux. He smiled at me, his teeth very white against his Riviera tan, his eyes blue as the Mediterranean outside the casino. He had chiseled features and a square, dimpled jaw like Captain America. His thick black hair gleamed under the lights and was slicked back, giving him the look of a Spanish flamenco dancer. It was no wonder he only slept alone by choice.

'May I buy you a drink?' he said, his English perfect but with a hint of a Parisian accent.

'No,' I replied. 'But I'll be happy to buy you one. I just made a killing at the wheel.'

He nodded. 'So I saw. You play here

often, *mademoiselle*?'

'You know I don't.'

My bluntness threw him for a moment. 'And why is that?'

'Well, first off I'm obviously American, which probably means I'm on vacation. And secondly, I have a feeling you're a pretty familiar face around here.'

He laughed, his voice a pleasant baritone, and asked me what I wanted to drink. I said a champagne cocktail and he ordered two. But when the bartender placed them before us, the man insisted on paying and to be honest I didn't put up much of a fight. It's been my experience that men like Alain Ardot liked their women beautiful and compliant, and since I wanted to get close to him I hid my normal in-your-face independence and did my best to appear impressed and available.

You see I was here to find my kid brother, Danny, who was on the run from Interpol and the Russian Mafia. His crime? He'd seen the mafia leader, Dmitri Kaslov, gun down a rival outside a New York restaurant and reported the murder to the police. The D.A.'s office had been after Kaslov for a long time and now saw their chance to nail him. Kaslov was arrested, booked, and a trial date was set. The only problem was the D.A. needed Danny to testify. Fearful of retribution, he'd been hesitant at first but after being assured by the police that he'd be protected, he'd finally agreed.

All his 'being a good citizen' effort got him was an attack on his life as he walked up the courthouse steps. Luckily, the shooter missed. He didn't make a second attempt but drove away before anyone could stop him. Scared, Danny took off and disappeared into the city. Now every cop and every Russian mobster in town was looking for him. But he'd stayed hidden and for several weeks even I didn't know where he was. By then I'd been diagnosed with leukemia and told that I only had a year at most to live.

Devastated, I promised myself that I'd find Danny and tell him before it was too late — for either of us. It took some doing and when I finally did catch up with him, I unintentionally led the cops and the mob guys to him. Furious, my brother fled before I could make him believe that I hadn't set him up or that my life really was on a short-string. Making matters worse was the fact that the D.A., angry at losing his key witness, issued a warrant for Danny, forcing him to skip the country.

I'd already traveled halfway around the world to find him, but so far had always been one step behind. Now, according to *D'Arc Investigations*, the French Detective Agency I'd hired to help me, two days ago one of their operatives had seen my brother waiting outside the Monaco train station. Danny, they said, had been picked up by a beautiful young brunette in a silver Maserati convertible, which the operative tailed but lost when an accident in the old section of the city tied up traffic.

Where did Alain Ardot fit in all this? The Maserati was registered to him. That didn't surprise me. Alain was a known playboy gambler who had shady contacts everywhere in Europe. He'd inherited a fortune from his late father, a media mogul, and his looks from his French actress grandmother who in her time rivaled Bridget Bardot in popularity. But being rich and handsome wasn't enough: he needed excitement and danger, and found it by hanging out with Europe's key underworld figures. I realized I was risking my neck by getting hooked up with him, but I also realized if anyone knew where my brother might be, it would be Alain Ardot.

The bar was jammed, forcing us to sit close together. I took advantage of it. As we got to know each other, I did my seductive best to encourage him to buy me two more cocktails. Maybe it's my Irish heritage or the fact that my dad could drink any man under the table, but I've always been able to handle my liquor — which when you're tall, green-eyed, have long red hair and are with a guy who has only one thing on his mind is a definite plus.

After we'd been at the bar for about a half-hour Alain finally got around to asking me to his villa. I stalled for a while, not wanting to appear too eager, and then halfway through my third cocktail excused myself and went to the ladies' room. There, hoping to make him become impatient, I took my time redoing my lipstick, then took a charm bracelet out of my silver clutch purse, fastened it about my wrist and returned to the bar.

My stalling had worked. Alain wasn't used to being treated this way, even by the supermodels he was always linked to, and looked irritated.

'Sorry for taking so long,' I said, downing my drink, 'but it was a zoo in there.'

He relaxed a little and offered me his hand. 'Shall we go then?'

'Of course.'

2

Alain's large Mediterranean villa clung to a steep hillside overlooking the harbor that seasonally was home to insanely expensive yachts owned by some of the richest men in Europe. It was old-world grand, with a red-tiled roof, whitewashed walls draped with pink bougainvillea, a cobblestone courtyard and breathtaking views in every direction. Built on three levels, it was high enough up the hill to see over the tops of the numerous high-rise office buildings, condominiums and a sprawl of shops and cafés that lined the downtown waterfront as well as most of the narrow winding streets that led inland, covering almost every inch of available real estate in an area no bigger than Central Park.

I had bittersweet memories of Monte Carlo. My ex-husband, Kirk Harmon and I had spent a week of our two-week honeymoon here, staying in one of the exclusive luxury suites in the prestigious Hotel de Paris before jetting off to ski in the Alps. At the time my boutique advertising agency in Manhattan was doing well, so I wasn't exactly a pauper myself. But I recall Kirk and I walking out of the hotel one morning to go sailing and having him point out all the gleaming Bentleys, Ferraris, Lamborghinis, McLarens and Aston Martins in the parking lot, most of them, he said, costing upwards of half a million dollars. I realized then that this was indeed the playground of the rich and famous.

Now, as I rode up the hill in Alain's metallic lime-green convertible Lamborghini Gallardo Spyder, with its 'Lambogreeny' vanity license plate, I blanked out all thoughts — bitter or sweet — of my short-lived marriage and concentrated on what I had to do once inside the villa. Getting information about Danny out of Alain wasn't going to be easy. He was only interested in a shortcut to the bedroom and stalling him long enough to find out if he knew where my brother was before leaving without warming his sheets was going to take some of my best 'Houdini' tactics.

It was a clear dark night, with a sickle moon and a warm breeze off the sea. Even though my penthouse in Manhattan has fabulous views of the city and the Hudson, I have to admit I was impressed by the panoramic view of Monaco, the yacht lights in the harbor, and the dark blue Mediterranean.

Alain parked in the courtyard and led me around the side of the house to a shimmering turquoise pool. Here his elegant white-coated valet stood beside an ice bucket containing a bottle of Gold Label Lanson champagne and two chilled, monogrammed crystal flutes. On seeing us, he popped the cork and set it on a white napkin.

'*Il'y a autre chose, Monsieur?*'

'*Non, merci. Bonne nuit*, Remi.'

The valet nodded politely to me and vanished into the villa.

'Pretty sure of yourself, weren't you?' I said to Alain.

'What makes you say that?'

I indicated the bottle. 'Or do you just happen to keep one of the best champagnes in the world iced and ready for any occasion?'

Alain laughed, removed his jacket and tie and threw them onto a chair before spinning the bottle around in the ice. 'I called Remi while you were in the powder room,' he admitted.

'Did I appear that easy?'

'Not at all. But as a gambler, one must always live in hope.'

'Or die in despair, as my ex is fond of saying.'

'Then you are not married?'

I held up my ring-less wedding ring finger. 'Not at this moment. You?'

He laughed again. 'Not at any moment.' He poured two glasses of champagne and handed me one. 'I hope my questions haven't offended you?'

'I'm from New York,' I said, amused. 'Does that answer your question?'

'Ah . . . then you're a fashion or a print model, yes?'

'No, neither. I'm in the advertising business.'

'I would not have guessed this,' he said, adding: 'Such a waste of beauty.'

'Keep it up,' I laughed. 'You're definitely winning me over.'

'No, no, I am serious. I have many friends in the modeling world — Paris, Milan, London — if you would like, I could introduce you to them.'

'Thanks, but no thanks. I hire models for my clients all the time in New York. I wouldn't swap places with them for anything. They're drop-dead gorgeous that's for sure. But I love to eat and drink and the idea of starving myself, or living on coke just to be thin enough to walk down a runway isn't my idea of fun.'

'And you like fun, yes?'

'I'm here, aren't I?' I looked at him, into his sea-blue eyes and realized it wouldn't be hard to put my shoes under this man's bed. He seemed to know what I was thinking because he leaned close and kissed me lightly on the lips.

I responded, but only enough to hold his interest. 'There's something you should know before we go any further.'

'Tell me.'

'I'm not just here for fun.'

He smiled, mockingly. 'I know.'

'You do?'

He nodded, sipped his champagne. 'You're trying to find your brother, Danny. Don't look so surprised,' he continued as my eyebrows arched. 'I have ears and eyes everywhere.'

'So it would seem.' I drank and felt the chilled bubbles tickling down my throat. 'If you knew that, Alain, why'd you invite me up here?'

'I wanted to see just how much he meant to you.'

'You've lost me.'

'To what extremes you'd go to find him.'

'Then you do know where he is?'

'I know someone who might.'

'The brunette in the silver Maserati?'

Now it was his turn to be surprised. He raised his glass in salute. '*Touché.*'

'Just who is she?'

'Michelle Boudreaux.'

'One of your many conquests, no doubt?'

'*Ma soeur.*'

'Your sister — you're kidding me, right? No,' I added, as he frowned, 'you're not kidding. But why doesn't she have your last name?'

'She doesn't want the world to know I'm her brother.'

'Mean you two don't get along?'

'No. We get along fine. But she's very independent and doesn't want to become successful because of me or my contacts. No, no, that's not true,' he corrected himself. 'Michelle's ashamed of me.'

I smiled wryly. 'But not enough to stop her from borrowing your Maserati.'

'It's actually hers now. She won it off me at baccarat.'

'Lucky *and* beautiful, that's not fair. What's her connection to my brother?'

'Perhaps you should ask her.'

'I'd love to. What's the catch — or should I say price?'

'Stay here for the night and in the morning I will arrange a meeting.'

I chuckled. 'It's tempting. But I think I'll pass. I would like one more glass of bubbly before you kick me out though.'

'You're that certain of yourself?'

'The more champagne, the more certain I get.'

Laughing, he picked up my glass, turned and took the bottle out of the ice. I quickly opened the back of the tiny gold giraffe that hung from my charm bracelet and dumped the contents into his champagne. The potent knockout drops, known as GHB, dissolved almost immediately.

He handed me my glass and I raised it in toast. 'To long platonic relationships.'

Amused, he touched my glass with his and we drank. 'I like your sense of humor, Jacqueline — '

'Jackie.'

'And I like you too. Are you absolutely sure you won't change your mind about staying?'

I hesitated, long enough to make him think I was undecided and then said: 'You're a very persuasive man, Alain. Drink up and I'll give it some more thought.'

We drank. For a little while he seemed fine. But as we finished our drinks and he went to refill them from the almost-empty bottle, I noticed his movements were sluggish and unsteady. He spilled the champagne as he tried to fill my glass and, confused and disoriented, gradually lost his balance and dropped the glasses. They shattered on the poolside concrete, glass flying everywhere. Alain frowned, as if trying to figure out what was wrong, and then plopped down on the nearest chaise longe. I studied him. He was not unconscious but incapable of functioning normally. It was time to act.

I hurried through the French doors and ducked into the villa. I looked around the room I was in. Back home it would have been called a den. The furniture was all wood and massive except for the long black leather couch. The Italian leather was soft as my cheek. I searched the room, looking for anything that might lead me to Alain's sister. The shelves were lined with books by famous authors and there was a beautiful antique mahogany desk in the far corner next to a widescreen television. I went to it and picked up the leather-bound address book sitting by the phone. *A. Ardot* was embossed in gold on the cover. Surprised that anyone still kept their phone numbers in a book rather than their cell, I opened the book to the page marked: B. I checked all the names. The fourth person down was Michelle Boudreaux. I scribbled her address, email and phone number down on a notepad, ripped out the page, closed the book and set it back beside the phone.

Outside by the pool Alain sat stupefied on the chaise longue. He looked at me but his glazed eyes told me he didn't see me. I took his car keys from the jacket on the chair and hurried around the side of the villa to the courtyard. The Lambo was still sitting there. Climbing in behind the wheel, I buckled up, fired the engine, found first gear and roared out through the gate.

3

The Lambo gripped the winding down-hill road like it was on rails. Driving it reminded me of something my ex was fond of saying: 'Irish, there are three things a man should experience before he dies: fast horses, fast cars and faster women.'

Well, I've never been interested in horses or women, but Alain's Lambo more than met the standard for fast cars and I had to admit that driving it was a thrill a second. I don't know how fast I was going. I was too busy wrenching the wheel this way and that to check the speedometer. But it was fast enough so that the buildings on both sides of me were nothing but a blur and the fat low-profile Pirellis squealed around every curve. Alain had adjusted the driver's seat so low I felt like I was eye-level with the road as it unwound before me in the headlights. Almost before I realized I was at the bottom of the hill. Ahead I could now see the main thoroughfares and, beyond, the yacht-lights glittering in the harbor.

I down-shifted, the V10 howling in protest, and slowing to about fifty, cut between two slower-moving cars and raced across *Boulevard Princesse Charlotte*. Traffic had thinned out a little at this late hour and after crossing two more wide streets I hung a left on *Avenue d'Ostende* and roared along the waterfront. I could already see the green dome of the casino in front of me and veering to my right followed *Avenue de Monte-Carlo* right to my hotel.

The entire trip had taken less than ten minutes. Pulling up in front of the colonnaded, red-carpeted entrance I turned the keys over to an attendant and hurried up the steps into the Hotel de Paris.

I've seen a lot of opulence in my life, but the extravagance of the magnificent lobby took my breath away every time I stepped into it. White marble gleamed everywhere. Statues, flower displays, elegant oriental rugs, a crystal chandelier hanging from the glass-domed ceiling, and the black statue of Louis XIV astride his horse that I always patted for luck on my way to the front desk — nothing had changed since my first stay here on my honeymoon. Except, of course, this time I wasn't with Kirk.

Crossing to the elevator, I rode up to the second floor. A party was going on in the suite next to mine. The door was open and rock music blared out. I walked past a man kissing a ravishing blonde in a pink shift that barely covered her golden body. His hands were unzipping her dress. By the time I'd unlocked my door the pink shift was down around the blonde's ankles and I realized she had no tan marks. Well, it *was* Monte Carlo.

Inside, my suite was sumptuously decorated in white and powder blue with a polished wood floor and a wrought-iron balcony facing the harbor. Leaving the light off, so that the living room was bathed in moonlight, I kicked off my heels and started for the bar. That's when

I walked past her.

I stopped, a step beyond the couch, for a moment not believing what I'd just seen, then did a double-take Hollywood would have been proud of.

It was a woman all right: a young, willowy, strawberry-blonde asleep with one arm tucked behind her head, the other hanging limply over the side of the couch above an empty, overturned cocktail glass.

Wondering who she was and how the hell she'd gotten into my suite, I leaned over her and gently shook the dangling arm. 'Hey, wake up . . . Come on,' I said when she didn't respond. 'Open your eyes, honey . . . C'mon, wake up, dammit!' I shook her arm harder but she only grumbled and tried to roll over. Slipping my arm around behind her back, I helped her to sit up. But her eyes remained closed and I could tell she wasn't with it.

'I hope you have better luck than I did,' a voice said behind me.

Startled, I gave a tiny gasp, dropped the girl and whirled around — to find a tall, slimly muscular man in a white terrycloth bathrobe watching me from the bedroom doorway. His thick dark hair was still damp from a recent shower and his aftershave smelled all too familiar.

'Sorry if I startled you,' he said, approaching. 'But I wasn't sure if I heard someone come in or not.'

I swore softly at him, using language that doesn't normally come out of my mouth.

'Wow,' he said, amused. 'You're really pissed, Irish, aren't you?' He went to the bar, opened the little refrigerator and took out two chilled glasses and a pitcher of vodka martinis. 'Here,' he said, filling the glasses, 'grab one of these. It'll help calm you down.'

I didn't want to be calm. I would have been much happier strangling him. For a few moments I couldn't find my voice. Then, throatily, I said: 'Kirk, you'd better have a goddamn good reason for being here, with her,' I thumbed at the girl, 'or I swear to God I'm going to call the *gendarmes* and have both of you thrown in the can!'

'You'd do that to your ex-husband?' he said mockingly. 'Someone who's flown all this way just to help you track down Danny?'

'You've got exactly one minute to find out,' I warned. I went to the bar, grabbed one of the cocktails and took a big gulp. It went down like cold liquid honey. 'So start talking.'

Kirk shrugged. 'There's nothing to talk about. I flew over to see how your search was going and if I could be of any help — '

'And just 'happened' to trip over Miss Goldilocks here while you were breaking into my suite, I suppose?'

'You're kidding but in fact that's pretty close to what actually happened. There's a party going on next door, as I'm sure you already know, and when I walked past the door she came running out, grabbed me and started kissing me — '

'Oh, pur-lease — '

'It's the truth. I pushed her away but she followed me, and collapsed outside your door.'

In the years I've known Kirk I've never

been able to tell when he's lying or telling the truth — including when I was married to him.

'All right,' I said, suspicious, 'then what happened?'

'I picked her up, carried her back to the party and came in here to take a shower.'

'Without a key?'

'I bribed the maid.'

'That I do believe. Then what? Just like that,' I snapped my fingers, 'Goldilocks magically reappears on the couch? Aw, come on, Kirk, you can do better than that.'

'Not unless I make up a story.' He added a green olive to the other martini and took a leisurely sip before adding: 'I must've left the door unlocked because when I came out of the shower, she was passed out on the couch.'

I sighed. Only a moron would make up a fairy tale like that and Kirk was no moron.

'Okay.'

'Okay?'

'Okay I believe you. Now get dressed, take her back to the party and then get the hell out of here. I'm beat.'

He looked hurt. 'Irish, you're not giving me much credit. Hell, don't you think I would've done just that if there wasn't any reason to keep her here?'

I yawned and wearily squeezed my brow. 'All right, I'll bite. What's the reason?'

Kirk took out a snapshot and gave it to me.

'Judas,' I said. 'Where'd you get this?'

'From Goldilocks' purse.' He went to the couch and picked up a gold clutch that I hadn't noticed before. 'I figured I'd call a cab for her . . . and then got curious . . . wondered who she was and if there was any reason I shouldn't get involved — '

' 'Involved'?'

'Yeah. You know. I'm well-known here, Irish. I've been coming to this hotel for years. If she's underage or wanted for some reason or other, I don't need to see my name plastered all over the media . . . just for trying to get some drunken party-girl home safely.'

I looked at the snapshot again. It

showed Danny in swim-trunks, pouring a bottle of champagne over the tanned naked body of the same girl on the deck of a luxury yacht anchored in the harbor. Both were laughing like drunken chimps.

I made a decision. 'Help me get her into the shower,' I told Kirk. 'I'll sober her up and maybe then we can find out if she knows where Danny is.'

4

A cold shower and two cups of room-service black coffee finally sobered up the girl. By then Kirk had gotten dressed and I'd checked the contents of her clutch. Wallet — cell phone — make-up — it contained nothing out of the ordinary. I examined her driver's license. It stated that Alita Corneau lived in Paris, was twenty-two, five foot four, and needed corrective lenses to drive. Since she wasn't wearing glasses I guessed she used contacts.

As she sat at the counter, wrapped in my bathrobe and sipping coffee, she didn't seem too delighted about being there; or being sober. She sullenly denied that Danny and she were friends, claiming that the only time she'd met him was at the party on the yacht and said she had no idea where he was now. I didn't believe her for a second; neither did Kirk. He warned her that she'd better alter her story and tell us the truth or we were going to have her arrested for breaking into my suite.

'I did not break in here,' Alita protested. Her English was stilted but otherwise surprisingly good. 'You, *monsieur*, carried me in here.'

'Sorry,' Kirk said. 'The only place I carried you was back to the party next door. Check with your friends if you don't believe me.'

'Then why am I here?' she demanded. 'I do not know either of you.'

I couldn't deny that but I still sensed she was lying. 'Do you remember kissing him in the hallway?' I asked, indicating Kirk.

She shook her head, 'I do not kiss strangers, *madame*. I am a model, not a *putain*,' and went on sipping her coffee.

Unfamiliar with the word I looked at Kirk, who mouthed 'whore' to me.

'Well . . . if that's your story, lady,' he said, 'then you're in trouble. As a lawyer I've no alternative but to call the police. Let's see if they believe you. If they do, you've got nothing to worry about. But if they don't — '

'I have plenty to worry about,' she cut in, and for the first time I saw fear in her lovely dark-blue eyes. 'More than you could possibly know.'

'Should've thought of that before you broke in here,' Kirk said heartlessly. He slipped me a sidelong glance as if to say, you take it from here, and playing Good Cop, I told him to hang on a minute.

'Look, honey,' I said, putting one arm about her shoulders, 'I'm on vacation and the last thing I need is to get involved with the police — it'll just take time away from the beach and the casinos. So how about we make a deal: You tell me where my brother is and you can walk out of here right now without anyone knowing a damn thing. Sound fair?'

She sipped her coffee as she thought about it and then shrugged. 'I do not know where your Danny is, and that is the truth.'

'But you do know someone who does?' Kirk said, probingly.

'Perhaps.'

'Give,' I said.

'Señor Vasquez, the man who owns the yacht.'

'Fernando Vasquez — the Spanish billionaire whose daughter just got engaged to that polo player from Buenos Aires?'

'*Oui*. Señor Vasquez invited Danny to the wedding.'

I couldn't believe it. My brother was no jet-setter and he definitely didn't travel in those kinds of super-rich circles.

'Listen,' I said, 'you must have Danny mixed up with someone else. My brother's trying to keep a low profile, not get his face in *People* Magazine!'

'Believe what you want,' Alita replied. 'But I do not mix things up. I hear this from Danny myself.'

'Okay, okay, I believe you. But he can stretch the truth at times. Is it possible that he was making all this up to impress you?'

She shook her head. 'I was there, at dinner on the yacht, when Señor Vasquez invited him.' I must have looked doubtful because she opened her clutch, took out her cell phone, tapping the screen several times, scrolling down until she found what she wanted. 'Here,' she said showing it to me, 'look.'

The photo showed Danny aboard a yacht, standing beside a short, balding man whom I'd seen many times on television: Fernando Vasquez.

I nodded, convinced, then on impulse said: 'What do you know about Michelle Boudreaux?'

Again I saw fear narrow Alita's eyes and realized I'd hit a nerve.

'Nothing.'

'Try again.'

She shrugged. 'Only that she is the sister of *Monsieur* Ardot.'

'You didn't know she was my brother's girlfriend?'

Alita laughed scornfully. 'That is absurd. Michelle would never . . . '

'Go on,' I said as she stopped. 'Never what?'

'Be serious about your brother.'

'Why not?'

'Because it is well-known that she prefers . . . women.'

'Oh, great,' I said. Then to Kirk: 'She's the one who picked my brother up at the train station — '

'In Ardot's Maserati,' Kirk finished. 'Yes, I know.' At my surprised look, he added: 'I'm the one who hooked you up with the detective agency, remember?'

Angry and tired, I said to Alita: 'New deal on the table.' I dug out Michelle's address. 'Show me where this is and we're all square. Agreed?'

She brightened. '*Je suis d'accord.*'

5

Kirk insisted on coming along — which was fine with me. Kirk travels only by private jet and limousine and who wouldn't rather sit in the comfort of a luxurious, chauffeured Mercedes Maybach than a bone-jarring, rattling French taxi that stinks of stale cigarettes?

According to the address I'd copied from Alain Ardot's address book, his sister lived in the penthouse of a high-rise condominium complex called Sea View Towers. Alita said it was only a few miles from the hotel, one of a row of white buildings on the waterfront with views of Larvotto Beach and, farther east, the border of Italy.

We drove along *Avenue Princesse Grace*, the mountains to my left, the Mediterranean on the right, until we reached the famed public beach. There we turned up a side street that led to the condo.

'Okay,' I told Alita as we pulled up to the entrance, 'you've done your part. You're free to go.'

She bit her lip nervously and didn't move.

'You heard her,' Kirk said. '*Allez!*'

'What's wrong?' I asked when she still didn't move. 'What're you afraid of?'

She avoided my eyes, said: 'It was not my fault.'

'What wasn't? What're you talking about?'

'Your brother — Danny — I told him not to go with her.'

'Her, who?'

'Wait a minute,' Kirk said. 'You mean Michelle?'

Her silence confirmed he was right.

'Was she on Vasquez's yacht with you? Goddammit, answer me,' he said, shaking her. 'Was Ardot's sister on that yacht with you and Danny?'

'*Oui.*'

I pushed Kirk's hands from her shoulders and turned her toward me, demanding: 'I need to know the truth and I need to know it now!'

She hesitated, teeth torturing her lower lip, then looked at me and said: 'Michelle is with the *Sûreté*.'

My mouth dropped and beside me even Kirk, who seldom is caught off-guard, looked surprised.

'You sure about that?'

'Positive. Though she'd deny it if you asked her.'

'Why?'

She hesitated, searching for the words in English, then said to Kirk: '*Agent de police banalise*.'

'She's an undercover cop,' he translated to me.

'What does she want with my brother?' I asked, almost knowing the answer before she told me. 'Any idea?'

'I've heard she is blackmailing him.'

'How?'

'She knows he is wanted by Interpol and is threatening to turn him in unless he pays her five million Euro.'

'That's over six million dollars,' I exclaimed. 'What is she, crazy? Danny doesn't have that kind of money.'

'Then he should never have told her he did,' Alita said.

'Is that what Michelle says or did you hear him yourself?'

'I hear him myself.'

I looked at Kirk. 'Why the hell would Danny do that?'

He shrugged and turned to Alita. 'Was he trying to impress her?'

She shrugged as if it was a foolish question. 'Of course, *monsieur*. Your brother,' she said to me, 'is very much in love with Michelle. He also knows she has many lovers — very rich lovers who could afford to lose that much on one spin of the wheel.'

I suddenly understood. 'Sounds like Danny. He never did like to be told no. I mean, what are a few lies when they get you what you want?' I looked at Kirk. 'Any suggestions?'

He looked at Alita. 'I don't mean to call you a liar, but you're really sure Michelle's with the *Sûreté*?'

'*Oui, monsieur.*' She thought a moment before adding: 'No one suspects it because of her brother's gambling and sometimes not-so-legal business dealings.'

'If she's blackmailing Danny, she's as crooked as Ardot!'

Alita shrugged but didn't reply.

I sighed, not sure what to do next. 'You any idea where Michelle took my brother?' I asked her.

She shook her head.

'Well, we're here now,' Kirk said, 'so why don't we make sure neither of them is in her condo. We've got to start somewhere, right?'

I nodded. 'Alita, how would you like to make some money?'

'Doing what?'

'Helping us find my brother.'

'Hey — whoa — hang on a minute, Irish,' Kirk said. 'Wouldn't you first like to know what kind of trouble our friend here's in?'

'Yes, I would. Well?' I said to Alita. Then as she remained silent: 'If it's got to do with money I'd be willing to help, or if you need a lawyer . . . ' I nodded toward Kirk. 'He's 'one of sorts'.'

It was an inside joke. Years ago when I first met Kirk I asked him what he did for a living and he replied: 'I'm a lawyer of sorts.' Now he just rolled his eyes.

'*Merci*. But the trouble I am in,' Alita said, 'you cannot help me with. But I will try to help you find Danny for as long as I can.'

'Deal.'

'But I do not want your money.'

'Suit yourself,' I said. Then including Kirk: 'Now, if either of you guys have any ideas how to get into this building so we can check out Michelle's condo, now would be the time to share them.'

'That is easy,' Alita said quickly. 'An old boyfriend of mine lives here. If he is home, he will let us in.'

It sounded too good to be true — either that or a big fat coincidence. And I don't believe in coincidences.

'Well, how convenient,' I said to Alita. 'How come you didn't mention this before?'

'I did not want to help you before.'

Kirk and I swapped looks.

'Well . . . do you want my help or not?'

'Lead the way,' I told her.

6

Mike Flynn, Alita's ex-boyfriend, was home and when the doorman called him from the front desk and explained that Alita and two friends from New York were in the lobby, he immediately said: 'Send 'em up!'

As we rode the elevator up to his condo on the sixth floor, I asked Alita to give us a quick run-down on Flynn. She shrugged and said that three years ago he'd worked in a real estate company in Belfast, and while on holiday here in Monaco had hit the jackpot playing Baccarat. She couldn't remember exactly how much money he'd won but it was enough to buy this condo and live comfortably here for the rest of his life.

'One last question,' Kirk said. 'What didn't you like about him?'

'Nothing. He is very nice. And most generous.'

'And your life is so terrific,' I said, 'that

you dumped him?'

She shrugged. 'He wanted to marry me and I do not want to get married. It is that simple.'

'My God, a girl after my own heart,' Kirk said.

I gave him a sour look that only made him chuckle. Then the elevator door opened and across the hallway, standing waiting for us in the doorway of his condo was Mike Flynn.

A big, fleshy man of about forty, in a rumpled white jumpsuit that set off his tan, he had curly red hair and an untrimmed red beard, a black patch over his left eye and when he grinned on seeing Alita, he reminded me of an overweight pirate.

He hugged her, lifting her off her feet and swinging her around until she insisted he put her down. He then pumped our hands as she introduced us and invited us in.

His spacious condo was a mess. Clothes lay everywhere as did books and magazines. Dirty dishes, glasses and silverware filled the sink. A half-empty bottle of Bushmills Irish whiskey and an empty tumbler sat on the kitchen countertop next to his laptop. The computer was on but in 'sleep mode.' The big flat-screen TV in the living room was showing a rerun of a World Cup soccer game with the sound muted. Flynn offered no apology for the mess, which scored points with me (I hate it when people apologize for being slobs), and taking his raincoat from the couch, asked us to sit down.

Before we could Kirk said: 'Thanks, but we can only stay a minute.' He looked at Alita. Picking up on his cue, she said: 'We're on our way to talk to a girlfriend of mine, and I just wanted to say hello and see how you were.'

'I'm fine, just fine, thank you,' Flynn replied, sounding disappointed. 'My Lord, but it's been a long time since I last saw you, pet. Almost a year is it not?'

'At least,' she admitted. 'Since that New Year's Eve party in Cannes, I think.'

'Aye . . . ' He sighed with regret, as if longing for the past, then turned to me:

'O'Hara, is it? Now there's a name that stirs an Irishman's heart. Were you by any chance born in the old country?'

I shook my head. 'South Boston,' I said. 'My ancestors came over during the potato famine.'

Kirk cleared his throat. 'We really have to be going,' he reminded.

'Of course,' Flynn said. Then to Alita: 'This friend you're visiting, who might she be? Could be I know her. I'm on speaking terms with most of the residents here.'

'Michelle Boudreaux,' Alita said, adding: 'Alain Ardot's sister.'

Flynn grinned lecherously. 'I'd *like* to know her, but so far, other than a polite nod or two, she's managed to avoid my clutches.' He laughed, went to the bottle and poured himself a drink. 'Are you sure you won't join me?' he asked us. 'There's plenty more where this came from.'

'Some other time,' I said. 'It's getting late and we really need to talk to Michelle.'

'Good luck with that,' Flynn said. 'She isn't around much these days. Rumor has it she's gone straight and has a boyfriend, an American by the way,' he added to me, 'and spends most of her time at his place.'

I dug out a photo of Danny and showed it to the Irishman. 'Would this be him?'

He took reading glasses from his pocket and studied the photo. 'Aye, I think it would. Though truth be told, I've only seen him once during the whole time Michelle's been dating him and that was just a glimpse as they were entering the lobby one day last week.' He raised his eyes from the photo and compared the two likenesses. 'He looks a lot like you, O'Hara. Would he be related by any chance?'

'My kid brother,' I said, tucking the photo away. 'Our father died recently and I'm trying to catch up with Danny so he can collect his share of the inheritance.'

Flynn nodded, 'I'm sorry for your loss,' and accompanied us to the door. There he kissed Alita on the cheek, adding: 'Don't be such a stranger, pet. I miss the good times together.'

Alita smiled, but didn't say anything.

Then all of us said good night and crossed the hallway to the elevator, where Kirk hit the button.

I didn't turn but sensed Flynn hadn't closed the door. Sure enough, when the elevator arrived and we stepped inside and faced him, he was still standing in his doorway, looking as sad and lonely as any Irishman I'd ever seen.

7

Michelle's penthouse suite had elegant, gold-trimmed white double-doors that faced the elevator. There was a peephole in the left-side door and gold-plated handle and buzzer on the right, suggesting that it was the only door that opened. Since Alita knew Michelle, earlier Kirk had suggested that our best plan was for her to try to get Michelle to willingly open the door.

'You can use the same excuse you used on Flynn,' he said. 'Only reverse it. If she's with the *Sûreté*, as you say, she probably knows you and Flynn were once an item, so coming over to visit him seems logical.'

'Yeah, but if she's got my brother with her,' I said, 'why would she want to expose him to someone who knows him? Wouldn't that blow her whole blackmail scam?'

Kirk frowned at me. 'If you've got a

better idea, Irish, I'm happy to listen to it.'

I didn't. Neither did Alita. So we went with his plan.

Now, as Kirk and I stayed out of the line of sight of the peephole, Alita pressed the buzzer and waited. No one answered. Alita pressed the buzzer again, longer this time but with the same result.

'Now what?' I said. 'Do we Rambo the door and risk that she has a silent alarm or come back another time?'

Kirk turned to Alita. 'You know Monaco better than any of us. How long do you think it'll take for the cops to respond?'

'Five maybe ten minutes. Unless,' she said softly, 'we turn the alarm off in thirty seconds.'

We both looked at her, half surprised, half suspicious.

'Thirty seconds?' I said. 'What's that — a time delay to give Michelle a chance to punch in the code to alert the alarm company that it's her?'

'*Oui*. And before you ask me,' she said,

seeing our expressions, 'yes, I have been here before.'

'And you didn't mention it because —?'

'I didn't want you to think I had anything to do with blackmailing Danny. He was sweet to me and I would never do anything to hurt him.'

'Why would I believe that now — or anything else you say?'

Kirk silenced me with a wave of his hand and confronted Alita. 'Just what the hell was or is your relationship with Michelle? You two lovers or something?'

'No.'

'Then how do you know about the alarm delay?' I asked.

When she didn't reply, Kirk said: 'I suggest you answer her.'

Alita sighed. 'It was my job to know.'

'Your job?' I said. 'What, you work for a security company?'

She hesitated, reluctant to share her secret.

'We're waiting,' Kirk said.

'I am a thief — a burglar — or was.'

I swear my mouth dropped. I know Kirk's did.

'You saying you had this place staked out?'

'*Oui.*'

Kirk swore under his breath. On a hunch I said: 'What about your Irish friend downstairs — are you two partners?'

'Were,' she admitted.

'But not now?'

'No.'

'How come you quit?' Kirk said. 'And don't tell me it's because you found religion.'

'No. God had nothing to do with it. I was almost caught during our last . . . ' She paused, searching for the right word.

'Heist?' I said.

'*Oui*, heist. I was trapped on the roof of a chateau near the Italian border, with my pockets full of stolen jewels, while below the *gendarmes* were searching for me. I was terrified. It was then I realized how afraid I was of going to prison.'

'So you called it quits?' Kirk put in.

She nodded.

'Is that the real reason you broke up with Flynn?'

'Yes.'

'Did he quit too,' Kirk asked, 'or is he still in business?'

'I do not know,' Alita said. 'He was very angry with me for quitting. Told me he had spent many months studying blueprints of the places we planned to rob — '

'He didn't seem angry tonight,' I said. 'So I guess he's forgiven you.'

'Perhaps. It has been more than a year since I told him — plenty of time to be more reasonable.' To Kirk, she added: 'If you agree, I can pick the lock, then run in and enter the code. That way, Michelle will never know we were there.'

Kirk rolled his eyes at me before saying: 'Help yourself.'

Alita took two lock-picks from her purse, poked them into the keyhole and deftly twisted them around until I heard a faint click. She then removed the tools, opened the door hurried inside. We followed and watched as she quickly punched in numbers on the wall keypad. 'The alarm has been shut off,' she explained. 'But it still would be wise to search quickly in case the *gendarmes* decide to speak to the owners anyway.'

'Is that likely?'

'It is not impossible.'

I glanced about me, noting that Michelle had good taste in furniture and art. Everything was starkly modern, with mostly black-and-white themes, and completely without feeling. It suggested the owner wasn't exactly warm and fuzzy . . . and I couldn't have lived there for a moment.

'Question,' I said to Alita. 'If you're no longer a thief or a cat-burglar, or whatever you call yourself, how come you're still carrying the tools of the trade around with you?'

She smiled. '*Les vielles habitudes sont difficile a casser.*'

Kirk chuckled. 'Old habits are hard to break,' he translated for me.

'Sounds less cliché in French,' I said, adding: 'I'll take this room. You search the master bedroom. You,' I added to Alita, 'check out the other bedroom.'

'What exactly is it we are looking for?' she asked as Kirk hurried into the master bedroom.

'Anything that belongs to Danny or might tell us where he is.'

We did not find any clues to my brother's whereabouts in any of the rooms. I did find a few bags of coke in the bathroom of the second bedroom; and Kirk found a framed photo of Michelle, topless and in a bikini bottom with one arm around the waist of an attractive blonde of about forty, in one of the bedroom drawers. I showed Alita the photo and asked if she knew who the woman was.

'But of course — that is Señora Vasquez.'

'Fernando's wife?'

'Uh-huh.'

'Is she bisexual?' Kirk asked, studying the photo.

Alita looked curiously at him. 'Isn't everyone, *monsieur*?'

8

After we'd finished searching the condo, we wiped our prints off everything we could remember touching and left. Alita stayed long enough to reset the alarm then closed the door behind her and joined us in the elevator.

We didn't speak until we were out of the building and driving away in Kirk's Maybach, then I asked Alita if Danny had ever said anything to her that suggested where he was living.

She looked annoyed. 'I've already said he didn't.'

'You've said a lot of things,' I reminded, 'most of them lies. So how about ditching your holier-than-thou attitude and answering my question?'

'It doesn't have to be an address,' Kirk put in. 'It could be anything. A casual remark . . . something he said that didn't mean anything to you at the time. Anything. Think, Alita. Think.'

She thought. The black, chauffeur-driven Maybach purred along the coastal road, its engine almost as quiet as our thoughts. The wind had sprung up and on the other side of the retaining wall white caps churned the surface of the sea.

Out the corner of my eye I could see Alita's profile. Her expression suggested she was trying to make a tough decision rather than trying to remember Danny's conversation.

'I know someone in the Criminal Division,' she said finally.

'How will that help us? Danny's wanted by Interpol and I was told that the Monaco police force is a member of Interpol. Won't that be sort of like inviting a cat to a canary party?'

'I trust this man,' she replied. 'And if you want my help, you must trust me.'

I sighed and shot Kirk a look, asking for his opinion. He nodded, just enough to tell me to play along.

'Okay,' I said. 'Go ahead. Contact him.'

Taking out her cell, she speed-dialed a number and listened. Someone must have answered because she began speaking in French. Kirk mouthed that he understood what she was saying.

Just before reaching the Hotel de Paris, Alita ended her conversation. Tucking her cell away she turned to me, saying: 'He will look into it.'

'How do you know this guy?' I asked.

'He arrested me once.'

'Charming.' I rolled my eyes at Kirk. 'How about we all meet in my suite tomorrow morning — say, about ten? I'll order breakfast.'

Kirk nodded and said to Alita: 'Any chance your friend will have some answers by then?'

'*Certainement.*'

The Maybach stopped in front of the hotel. Kirk told the chauffeur to take Alita home and then he and I got out.

'See you tomorrow morning,' I told Alita. 'Good night.'

She smiled, a bit nervously I thought, and then the big black Mercedes pulled away.

Kirk and I watched it join the late-night traffic heading into town.

'Think we'll ever see her again?' I asked Kirk.

'No.'

'Me neither.' I yawned, adding wearily: 'Christ, I'm getting so damn tired of this.'

He smiled, sighed, put his arm around my shoulders and pecked me on the cheek.

'Getting old's a bitch, ain't it?'

I was too tired to even laugh.

★   ★   ★

Kirk showed up at my hotel suite at nine-thirty the next morning. I'd already called room service and asked them to deliver breakfast for three at ten o'clock. I added that they could send the coffee up right away and was sitting drinking a cup out on the balcony when Kirk arrived. He poured himself a cup, added sugar and cream and sat across the white wrought-iron table from me. It was overcast but the view of the Mediterranean and the harbor was still spectacular and we sipped our coffee in meditative silence.

Ten o'clock arrived and with it a waiter

pushing a wheeled cart containing our breakfast. I'm not much of a breakfast eater — a piece of toast, OJ and coffee is about my limit — but Kirk wolfed down his scrambled eggs, bacon and sweet rolls like he hadn't eaten in a month.

'How the hell do you stay so trim?' I said, enviously watching him eat. 'My God, if I ate like that every morning I'd put on a hundred pounds.'

'Not if you worked out regularly.'

'I run three times a week, what the hell do you call that?'

There was a knock on my door. 'Better late than never,' I said, rising. I went to the door and opened it, expecting to see Alita: instead two men in gabardine raincoats confronted me. The older and smaller of the two, a distinguished-looking man of forty whose graying black hair showed beneath his dark-blue beret, explained they were Homicide Detectives with the Monaco Police Department and flashed ID to prove it. With an uneasy heart, I invited them in and led them out onto the balcony.

Introducing them to Kirk, I asked them

to join us for coffee.

They declined and remained standing. The older detective asked me if I knew a young woman named Alita Corneau. Kirk gave me a look that warned me to keep quiet, and then replied: 'As Ms. O'Hara's lawyer, I must ask you to address all your questions to me, gentlemen.'

The younger, larger man grew hostile and said something in French.

'He says they can always officially question us at the station, if we prefer,' Kirk said to me. He smiled sweetly at the detectives. Then spoke rapidly in French to them. The older detective swallowed, hard, but managed to keep calm as he spoke to Kirk.

Kirk let him finish then said to me, 'Routine cop questions: they want to know if we were together last night, and if so, where were we.'

'What'd you tell them?'

'Squat really. Just that we gambled some, went for a drive up the coast, then came back here and went to bed.'

'Separately or together — as if I need to ask?'

'Hey, Irish . . . a man has to protect his manly image.'

'In other words, you stayed over?'

Kirk grinned. 'Well, we are in France.'

Before I could reply, the older detective looked at me and in English, said: 'Is it true that this gentleman was once your husband?'

'Absolutely.'

'At any time were you with Alita Cordeau last night?'

'Before I let her answer that,' Kirk said, 'is Alita alive or dead?'

'*Mort,*' the younger detective said grimly.

I didn't need a translation for that. But I did need a moment to recover from the shock. Then I indicated the third place setting at the table, saying: 'Well, as you can see, we were expecting her to join us for breakfast. So that hardly makes us suspects.'

'She was with us until about three in the morning,' Kirk said sharply. 'Then I told the driver to take her home.'

'Ah,' the older detective said. 'Then

you cannot say for certain that he obeyed you?'

'No. He came with the car, recommended by the rental office. Here,' Kirk dug out his wallet and extracted two business cards. 'One's mine, the other is *Côte d'Azur* Rental — call 'em. They specialize in high end luxury cars. I'm sure someone there will verify the paperwork for you — a new Maybach. Under my law-office name.'

'How was she killed?' I asked.

'I did not say she was killed,' the older detective said.

'No, you didn't,' I replied. 'But I doubt if you'd be bothering us if she happened to have a heart attack.'

'She was strangled, *madame*.'

'You want us to identify the body?' Kirk asked. 'We'll be happy to.'

'It is not necessary, *m'sieur*. I have already done that myself.'

The statement seemed to upset the younger detective. He spoke in French to his partner. I couldn't understand what he said, but it made the older detective frown and he motioned for him to be quiet.

Kirk said: 'Any other questions, *m'sieurs*?'

'How long had you known her?'

'Just since last night.' He went on to explain briefly about the next-door party and how he'd carried Alita back to it, only to have her show up again on my couch while he was showering.

'So you would have us believe that you invited a stranger, someone you'd just met along for a drive?'

'She was lonely,' Kirk said, his sarcasm making the older detective flush with annoyance.

The younger detective spoke to Kirk in French. Kirk answered him and then continued talking to both detectives in French for several minutes. Whatever he told them seemed to satisfy them. The older detective then gave me his card, told me to notify him before I actually left Monaco and then he and his partner were shown out by Kirk.

'What did you tell them?' I said when he rejoined me on the balcony.

'Basically the truth. That you had cancer and were trying to find your brother to tell him the news.'

'Did they say if they had any idea who killed Alita?'

'No. But maybe that's because her body's disappeared.'

' 'Disappeared'?'

He shrugged. 'That's what the young guy said. I think he wanted to question us about it, but his partner shut him down.'

'So that's what that little exchange was about,' I said, remembering. Then: 'I wonder who the hell stole the corpse?'

'Good question. By the way,' he said, 'before I forget, I'm flying out of here this afternoon.'

'Back home, you mean?'

He nodded. 'I'll grab a chopper to Nice and fly back to New York from there.'

'Isn't that kind of sudden?'

'Not really. I've had these meetings set up for some time. I just needed Jeanine to lock down the dates.' He reached out and pressed his hand fondly over mine. 'I'd feel a lot better, Irish, if you'd come with me.'

'Sorry. I have to find Danny — hopefully before Michelle Boudreaux turns

185

him over to Interpol. Can't you postpone the meetings — stay another day or two?' I added.

'You know I would if I could.' When I nodded, he said: 'At least let me tell the Detective Agency to assign you a bodyguard.'

'Thanks,' I said. 'I've seen that movie. Don't worry, I'll be okay.'

He grunted, 'Sure you will,' and went on wolfing down his breakfast.

'Judas,' I said. 'You could at least *pretend* you've lost your appetite.'

9

That afternoon I said goodbye to Kirk outside the hotel. Awaiting him was the chauffeured Maybach that was taking him to the heliport in nearby Fontvieille, where he'd catch a shuttle 'copter to the *Côte d'Azur* Airport in Nice. It was only a seven minute flight but for some reason I was worried about his safety. It was a needless worry because he was fully capable of looking after himself almost anywhere in the world. But it made me realize that even though we were divorced I still cared for him.

'Call me when you land in New York,' I said. 'Let me know you're safe.'

'Will do.' He pecked me on the cheek. 'Take care of yourself, Irish. And remember, whoever these people are, they play for keeps. So don't underestimate them.'

'I won't.'

'And if you so much as think you're

being tailed, call the agency and tell them you want a bodyguard — twenty-four-seven. Can't be too careful, you know, especially after what happened to Alita.' He climbed into the rear of the luxurious Mercedes and waved at me through the window. I waved back and watched as the big black car glided away.

As it disappeared in traffic I turned to enter the hotel — and caught a glimpse of a tall young man in a gray suit as he quickly turned away so I couldn't see his face. I sensed he'd been watching me and I went cold for a moment. He was standing on the sidewalk, less than twenty paces from me, and guessing he wouldn't shoot me in view of everyone entering and exiting the hotel, I started toward him. Spooked, he hurried across the street and was soon lost in the crowd of happy, noisy, sunburned middle-aged tourists who'd just come off one of the cruise ships.

I stopped and looked around to see if I could see anyone else who might be watching me — but no one looked suspicious and I entered the hotel. It too was mobbed and unable to think of what to do next, I headed for the elevators. There were several guests waiting there to go to their rooms. As I stood at the rear of them I felt a hand grip my arm and before I could protest, a man's voice whispered behind me: 'Come with me — quietly.'

I obeyed and felt myself led toward the door marked: *Escaliers*. I felt something hard pressed in my back and guessed it was a gun. I tried to see what the man looked like but he kept directly behind me and, opening the door, I stepped on through. The stairwell was empty and quiet enough so I could hear my heart thudding.

'All right,' the man said, his French-accented voice sounding vaguely familiar. 'Turn around.'

I obeyed and saw it was the man in the gray suit I'd seen outside. Now that I could see his face I recognized him as the younger detective who earlier had been so hostile toward Kirk and me. I also realized that the gun in my back had actually been his finger and couldn't help

189

feeling embarrassed.

'What the hell . . . ' I began.

'I am sorry if I frightened you, *madame*, but I need to talk to you.'

''Bout what?'

'Alita Corneau.'

'Go on.'

'She called me . . . earlier . . . asking me to help you.'

I couldn't hide my surprise. 'You're the 'friend' she was talking about?'

'*Oui.*'

'Christ, why didn't you say something before — when you and the other detective were in my room?'

'I trust no one,' he said.

'Not even your partner?'

'No. Nor can I be seen with you unless it is official police business.'

'Then how are you going to help me?'

He hesitated before saying: 'It is possible I know where your brother is hiding.'

My heart skipped. 'Where?' Then before he could answer: 'Take me to him. Please.'

'I will. But not now. Tonight, when it is dark — '

'That may be too late. Alita said Michelle threatened to hand Danny over to Interpol unless — '

'You must trust me.'

'That's what Alita said, and look where it got her — '

He said impatiently: 'I will meet you outside this address at eight o'clock. Do not be late.' He shoved his card into my hand, turned and pushed out through the door.

The name printed on the front was: *Inspecteur Claude A. Bonfils*. I turned the card over and saw an address scribbled on the back. It was in nearby Fontvieille, one of the four districts that made up the principality of Monaco, and I wondered if my brother was really hiding there or if I was being sucked into a trap.

10

That night a taxi let me off one block from the address that was on the back of Inspector Bonfils' card. I was fifteen minutes early. My plan was to check out the area for any suspicious or threatening types, thereby giving myself a better chance of surviving — if it was a trap. I know this sounds paranoid but at this point, I, like Bonfils, trusted no one.

Keeping to the shadows, I moved quietly along the sidewalk and soon came in sight of an old three-story, red-stucco residence facing the Port of Fontvieille. The large harbor was filled with luxury yachts and sailboats, and on the other shore loomed the massive, flat-topped rock on which the old village of Monaco-Ville and the royal palace were built. I took my time, pausing each time I drew level with an alley or another side street to make sure no one was lurking there. I was the only person on the street that I could see, but as I got within a few doors of the residence, a late-model, black Citroën sedan with tinted windows pulled up. I stopped, wishing at that moment I had a gun, and then relaxed as Inspector Bonfils got out.

He nodded politely to me, saying, 'This way, please,' and led me to a dark, empty alley that ran alongside the red house. We entered the alley and halfway along it stopped in front of a side entrance. Bonfils turned to me, his tone grim as he said: 'Officially, this is as far as I can go.'

'How about 'unofficially'?'

'Either way, I'm afraid you are on your own from here, *madame*.'

I shrugged. 'Okay. Thanks for helping me this much.' I went to open the door, then stopped and looked at him. 'Answer me this: Alita said that Michelle Boudreaux, who allegedly kidnapped my brother, is a member of the *Sûreté*. Do you know if that's true?'

'Not to my knowledge, no.'

'Could she be what we in America call

an undercover cop and you don't know about her?'

'This I very much doubt.'

'Why would Alita say that then?'

He shrugged. 'I have no idea.'

I don't know why but I sensed he was lying. 'If my brother is in there and being held against his will, surely that's a crime even in Monaco?'

'Of course.'

'Then why won't you go in with me — officially or unofficially? I mean you must think Danny's in there or you wouldn't have gone to all this trouble to get me here?'

He sighed, as if he'd like to help me but was trapped by bureaucracy.

'Thanks anyway!' I snapped and reached for the door handle.

'Wait,' he said. Then as I turned to him: 'To catch a shark one must sacrifice a smaller fish — '

I looked incredulously at him. 'You saying you're using my brother as bait?'

He turned without answering and hurried off along the alley.

'You bastard!' I hissed after him.

Ignoring me, he left the alley and within a few moments I heard his car start and pull away.

★ ★ ★

Opening the door I stepped inside and found myself in a little entryway. It was dark but I could make out stairs leading up to the main house and, to my right, more stairs descending to what I guessed was the basement. I keep a pencil flashlight in my purse at all times in case I get a flat on a dark road or highway some night and need to put on the spare. Fumbling it out, I aimed it at the floor and turned it on.

At the bottom of the steps was a closed door. I quietly descended to it and tried the handle. The door opened and, keeping my flashlight aimed ahead of me, I entered a large, damp-smelling room. It was filled with old furniture and junk. But there was no sign of Danny.

Disappointed, I turned to leave — then stopped as I saw a tall, darkly handsome man standing in the doorway holding a gun.

'Y-You?' I exclaimed, recognizing him instantly. 'Christ, I should've known you'd be mixed up in this.'

Alain Ardot grinned and wagged the gun at me. 'Ladies first.'

I walked around him and together we climbed the stairs and walked out into the lighted hallway beyond.

11

Continuing on down the hall, we passed between two closed doors and then stopped at the door at the end. Alain knocked three times and waited. Within moments I heard a key turn in the lock and the door opened to reveal another familiar face.

I laughed bitterly. 'Judas, this is turning into old home week.'

'Nice to see you too,' Mike Flynn chuckled. He stepped back so we could enter.

I walked a few steps into the large, empty, high-ceilinged living room, then stopped and turned to Alain. 'If my brother is here, I'd like to see him.'

'I'm afraid that's impossible,' a voice said behind me. I whirled around, just in time to see a slender, stunningly attractive woman step out of a back room. She had sultry, dark, almond-shaped eyes and long dark hair that fell loosely about her beautiful face. I recognized her from the photo in her condo and understood immediately why Danny was hooked on her.

'Finally,' I said, trying to keep calm. 'I was beginning to think we'd never meet.'

'There was no need,' Michelle Boudreaux said in perfect English, ' — up till now.' She offered me her slim tanned hand. 'Welcome to my home, Ms. O'Hara.'

Ignoring her hand, I said: 'Where's Danny?'

'Safe.'

'That doesn't tell me much.'

'Your brother is fine.'

'For how long — till you milk him for five million?'

She frowned. 'I see you've been talking to Alita. That is a dangerous mistake. She is full of bitterness and lies.'

'Was,' I corrected. 'She's dead. But of course, you already know that, don't you?'

'I did not kill her, if that's what you're suggesting.'

'But you know who did, I'll bet.'

Mike Flynn said impatiently: 'Quit stalling, dammit. Tell her the truth, Michelle. If you don't, I will.'

'I already know the truth,' I said. 'You,' I told Michelle, 'are a crooked cop who's holding my brother for ransom and you,' I added to Flynn, 'plan burglaries but don't have the balls to rob the places yourself so you used Alita, and God knows who else, to take the risks for you — which pretty much sums you up as a gutless leech.'

'What about me?' Alain asked, amused. 'Don't I get to be on your hit list?'

Before I could answer, a voice behind me said: 'Do not forget about me either, madame.'

I turned and saw Inspector Bonfils, who'd just entered from the hall and was now watching me from the doorway.

I shook my head, disgusted. 'Shame on me,' I said. 'I should've known better than to trust a weasel like you.'

He shrugged, closed the door and joined the others.

'So what happens now?' I asked. 'You going to kill me like you did Alita and, for all I know, maybe Danny too — '

Michelle cut me off. 'Your brother is not dead.'

'I'm supposed to take your word for that?'

'It is the truth. Danny is alive and . . . safe.'

'Which is more than he deserves to be,' put in Flynn, 'considering the amount of trouble he's caused us.'

'Caused you?' I snapped. 'Don't you have that ass-backwards? I mean he's the one who was kidnapped and being held for ransom!'

Michelle gave a weary sigh, rolled her eyes at the others, and then said to me: 'We did not kidnap Danny or demand any ransom. He is being held in protective custody in order to save his life.'

'So that's what they're calling it now?' I said.

'Save your sarcasm,' Alain said. 'Michelle's telling you the truth. Danny double-crossed a major drug dealer in Cannes named Julien LaSalle, a man responsible for at least a dozen murders this year alone.'

'Your brother would be dead by now,'

Flynn said, 'if she hadn't risked her neck to get him out of there — '

'Yes, and in doing so,' Michelle said, 'I sacrificed six months of undercover work as one of his girls — '

'What're you talking about?'

'Pretending to be a pusher was the only way of learning how his drug operation works,' she said angrily.

'Now all that work's not only gone down the drain,' Bonfils said, 'but because she put Danny's life ahead of the sting, Michelle may be suspended from the *Sûreté*.'

I looked at the four of them incredulously. 'You really expect me to believe this fairy tale you're spinning me?'

'It's not a fairy tale.'

'Sure sounds like one from where I'm standing. I mean I know my brother. He's no candidate for good guy of the month. Truth is he's selfish and a liar and if you say he was mixed up with a drug dealer, that doesn't surprise me at all. Still he's my brother. I love him and because I'm not going to be around for long, I want to make my peace with him. But you,' I added to Michelle, 'aren't family. And the idea that you'd be willing to risk your life and sabotage your career on account of someone of Danny's caliber — well, sorry, guys, I just can't buy that. So unless there's more to this than you're letting on — '

'There is,' Bonfils cut in, 'but we can't reveal what it is right now.'

'A 'need to know', is that it?' I gave an ugly laugh. 'Christ, can't you guys come up with something less cliché than that? How naïve do you think I am?'

'Calm down,' Flynn said. 'Try to see this from our point of view.'

'Why? Danny isn't your brother, he's — '

'Look,' Bonfils interrupted, 'we know this is hard for you. And we know what we're asking sounds callous. But all we want you to do is back off and stop looking for him for a little while.'

'A few days at most,' said Flynn. 'Just long enough for us to wrap this up and crack Julien's drug ring.'

''Us'?' I snorted. 'You're a cop too?'

'No,' he said soberly. 'I'm not. But I am

with Interpol. And,' he added as my mouth dropped, 'I do know that Julien's connected to most of the other drug dealers throughout Europe and the Soviet Union, and by shutting him down we'll be serving notice that we're really serious about our war on drugs.'

I took a deep breath and let it out slowly. I was having a hard time swallowing what I'd just heard. Yet they all seemed so sincere. 'What's your role in all this?' I asked Alain. 'I mean, you don't have the cleanest image in town. I've heard you're linked to drugs too — and that's not counting that you're a womanizer, gambler and playboy extraordinaire.'

'Guilty on all counts,' he said quietly. 'But I do what I do for my own personal pleasure, not at the expense of others. I don't *deal* in drugs. Nor do I have pushers selling drugs to school kids or pimps turning young girls into whores.'

'Even if I believed that,' I said, 'and I'm not saying I do, that still doesn't prove the rest of you guys wear White Hats — or that you didn't kill Alita.'

Michelle and Bonfils exchanged looks,

as if asking each other a silent question, they both looked at Flynn.

'What reason would any of us have to kill her?' he asked me.

'How about that she wouldn't do your dirty work anymore?'

He laughed. 'So you bought into her story of me being a master criminal, eh?'

'Till you give me a reason not to, why shouldn't I?'

'I already gave you one — I'm with Interpol.'

'Got any proof of that?'

Flynn dug out his wallet and held it up so I could see his Interpol I.D.

'Okay,' I said. 'I believe you. But if you guys didn't kill Alita, who did?'

'We don't know,' Michelle said.

'We're still looking into it,' Bonfils added. 'Unfortunately, with her corpse disappearing before the coroner could examine it, a lot of clues will go unsolved.'

'But you already said she was strangled.'

'No. That is what my partner said. All I saw were marks on her throat that suggested she was strangled. It is not the same.'

'This much we do know, though,' Flynn said. 'Alita was not a small-time thief or a cat-burglar, like she claimed.'

'Go on.'

He shrugged. 'That's all we know for sure.'

'It's possible,' Michelle said after a pause, 'that she was an assassin.'

Remembering Alita, and how frightened she'd seemed when she was with Kirk and me, I could only shake my head and say: 'No way. Party girl, high-priced hooker maybe, but assassin — never.'

'You may be right,' Michelle said. 'As of now we don't have any concrete proof that's she's a paid killer, or any idea who she's working for.'

On impulse, I said: 'How about Fernando Vasquez?'

'The billionaire?'

I nodded.

'Why him?'

'Alita knew him well enough to be invited on board his yacht.'

'She told you that?'

'Didn't have to. She showed me a photo she'd taken with her cell of Danny standing on deck with Vasquez.'

Michelle hesitated, swapped looks with Bonfils and Flynn, then asked me: 'Did Alita ever say anything to you, or your lawyer friend Kirk Harmon that suggested she was working for Señor Vasquez?'

'Mean as an assassin?'

'As anything?'

'Uh-uh. Said she knew him, and was at the party on his yacht, same as Danny, but nothing else.'

None of them spoke. But I guessed their brains were in high-gear.

'For the record,' I said to Michelle, 'when I mentioned your name to her, she sort of came unglued — as if she was nervous or afraid of you.'

Michelle absorbed what I said then sighed wearily. 'Do you still want to see your brother?'

'More than anything.'

'Then come with us.'

12

With Michelle leading the way, we left the house. Outside, Alain and Flynn went their own way while I, Michelle and Inspector Bonfils got into his car and drove toward the harbor.

The drive was all downhill and it only took a few minutes to reach the waterfront. Traffic was heavy and everywhere people were enjoying the evening. Bonfils parked in a restricted area by the retaining wall and the three of us went through a gate and down some steps to one of the docks. Expensive yachts and sailboats were tied up in slips that jutted out into the harbor. Loud music and laughter was coming from some of the yachts and I saw guests partying on-deck. The tide was coming in. The boats rocked gently on the swells and I could hear the water slap-slapping against their hulls.

We walked to the end dock and then out onto the slip, stopping only when we reached the last yacht. It wasn't as grand as some of the yachts moored there, but it was still large enough to impress me. All the lights were off on board, which seemed to trouble Michelle and Bonfils. They spoke rapidly in French. Then telling me to wait on the slip, the two of them drew their guns and quietly stepped aboard.

I watched as they moved stealthily to the main cabin. I lost them in the shadows then picked them up again as they reached the door, inched it open and ducked inside. I stood there, worried about my brother's safety and wishing I could do more for him. I hadn't long to wait. Bonfils soon reappeared and beckoned to me to come aboard. Obeying, I asked him what was wrong and if Danny was all right.

Before he could answer Michelle joined us. 'Your brother's gone,' she told me.

'He's taken off, you mean?'

'Kidnapped.'

'Christ.' Something cold dropped in my stomach. 'Are you sure?'

'*Oui*. Whoever grabbed him also shot

the two detectives guarding him.'

'Any idea who the kidnapper was?' I asked numbly.

She shook her head. I saw a different answer in her lovely dark eyes.

'You're lying.'

'No, we honestly don't know,' Bonfils put in. 'But whoever it was must've known the detectives — and maybe your brother too.'

'Why do you say that?'

'Because,' Michelle said grimly, 'that's the only way they could've gotten close enough to have killed them.'

I shut my eyes for a moment, trying to control my emotions. 'Surely that narrows down the suspects?'

'Drastically. Trouble is,' she said, 'the person everything points to is . . . dead.'

'You mean Alita?'

Michelle nodded. 'I'm sorry,' she said. 'I feel responsible for your brother's abduction. I promised him protection and didn't live up to my word. I promise you this, though,' she added, 'no matter what it takes I'll find Danny and arrest whoever's responsible.'

She seemed genuinely sorry and I sensed she meant what she said, but frankly that didn't make me feel any better. I sat glumly silent in the back seat of Bonfils' Citroën as he drove Michelle and me to my hotel. There, after getting out, I made them swear that they would contact me the moment they had any news about Danny.

Entering the lobby I checked at the front desk to see if there were any messages for me. There was one; it was from Kirk, asking me to call him on his private line. I rode the elevator up to my room, grabbed the phone and called him. He answered on the second ring and came straight to the point:

'You'll never guess who called me.'

'Danny?'

'Alita.'

'Alita? That's impossible. She's dead, remember?'

'Apparently not.'

'You sure it wasn't someone impersonating her?'

'Yep. It was her all right. When I asked her to prove who she was, she repeated everything we did last night — right down to our conversation with Flynn, breaking into Michelle's condo and the code for the alarm. It was definitely her, Irish.'

'If that's true, why would the cops claim she was dead?'

'I asked her the same thing.'

'And?'

'She says it's all part of some massive cover-up.'

'By whom?'

'Certain people in the *Sûreté* and Interpol — maybe even the local cops — even she wasn't sure exactly how far the corruption had spread.'

'And you believed her?'

'Not at first. But then she reminded me how her body 'conveniently' disappeared after she'd been identified.'

'I'm not following you.'

'Remember those two detectives who came to your hotel room, asking us questions about Alita?'

'Sure. What of it?'

'The young one wanted to question us about how her corpse vanished, remember, and — '

'Sure, and you said his partner wouldn't let him. So what?'

'According to Alita, he's one of them — the older detective, I mean. He's been on the take for years. Evidently,' Kirk added before I could say anything, 'Michelle, Alain and God knows who else are involved with some big-time drug dealer in Cannes — '

'Julien LaSalle, yes, I know. They say they're out to nail him. I think Danny's somehow involved, too,' I added.

'Danny? You're kidding? What the hell's your brother doing mixed up in a major drugs bust?'

'I hate to think. But according to Michelle, whom I've just spent the last few hours with — her, Alain and that young detective, Inspector Bonfils — LaSalle's pissed at Danny and maybe even has a hit out on him.'

'Jesus-Joseph-Mary!'

'I know. And it gets worse. Michelle and Bonfils had Danny stashed in a safe-house — a yacht in the Fontvieille marina — but when we got there about an hour ago, he was gone — kidnapped.' I paused, fighting tears and my emotions, then added: 'I was going to call you as soon as I got to my room here to see if you could help me track him down, but then I got your message and . . . ' I broke off, tears welling, and expelled all my frustration and fears in a long dejected sigh.

'Take it easy, Irish,' Kirk said gently in my ear. 'I'll call my pilot soon as I hang up and — '

'No, no, don't do that,' I broke in. 'Flying over here won't help.'

'It'd give you a shoulder to lean on, if nothing else.'

'Thanks. That's sweet of you. But honestly, I'm all right. But I would like you to check around over there and see if anyone you know has the eyes or ears to the ground in Monaco — '

'What about *D'Arc* — have you talked to any of their investigators — to see if they can find Danny?'

'No. I told you. I just walked in. Besides, they won't know anything. My God, they didn't even know Danny had been stashed on that yacht, let alone that he's now been kidnapped.'

'So, what're you going to do?'

Before I could answer I heard someone knocking. 'Hang on,' I told Kirk, 'there's someone at the door. Be right back.' I put the receiver down and went to the door. Deciding to see who it was before I opened it, I peered through the tiny viewing hole.

The face that stared back at me rocked my senses.

13

Quickly returning to the phone, I told Kirk I'd call him later and hung up. I then opened the door, allowing Alita to enter. 'Nice to see you're back with the living.'

'I'm sorry I couldn't let you know earlier,' she said, 'but playing dead was the only way I could save my life and Danny's.'

'It was you who snatched him off the yacht?'

'But of course.'

'Then you know where he is now?'

'*Oui.* But I cannot take you to him.'

'Why the hell not?'

She hesitated, obviously uncertain about what to say next.

'Wait a minute,' I said, catching on. 'It's Danny, isn't it? He doesn't want me to know where he is because he's afraid I want him killed — right?'

She nodded, looking miserable. 'I am

sorry, Jacqueline, but he would not go with me unless I gave him my word.'

'I understand . . . ' I sighed wearily. 'Look, what happened wasn't my fault. Dmitri Kaslov, who runs the Russian Mafia in New York, had his men follow me without my knowing, and I led them right to my brother. They tried to kill him, but the cops showed up and during the shootout that followed, he managed to escape. He's been on the run ever since and blames me for betraying him.'

'I know. This Danny told me. I tell him I think he is mistaken and explain that you and your friend, Mr. Harmon, had treated me well. But Danny, he is stubborn, as you know, and . . . well . . . ' She shrugged.

I nodded, understanding, and said: 'Then why are you here — if you didn't come to take me to Danny, I mean?'

'He needs money — cash — but is afraid to use his debit card for fear that Julien LaSalle's men or Interpol might trace him through it. He's also afraid they have the banks staked out, which means he only has you to turn to for cash.'

I don't know why but I sensed she was lying, or that my brother had lied to her and she didn't know it. 'What about his friend, Señor Vasquez? Is Danny afraid he'll turn him in if he asks for a loan?'

'He already borrowed money from Señor Vasquez, and can't ask for more.'

I looked at her and she immediately lowered her eyes uneasily.

'Alita, I have to tell you, I get the feeling you're not telling me everything you know. I mean, Danny could give you his debit card and his password, and you could take out as much as he wants from his account.'

She shifted uncomfortably, looked at the carpet for another moment then looked at me, saying: 'There is no money in his account.'

'He told you that? 'cause if he did, he's lying to you. He inherited a lot of money, just like I did, and unless he's splurged on a couple of yachts or thrown it all away gambling, I very much doubt that he's broke.'

Again she hesitated, this time absently toeing the floor as she asked: 'So you will not give him any money?'

'No. Not one cent. Tell him I'm willing to help him all I can — even pay off his gambling debts, if that's the problem. But I won't give him any cash. It'd just be throwing away good money after bad.'

Alita sighed, frustrated by my answer, then said: 'What if he paid you back ten times more than you loaned him — would you then agree?'

'Nope. Not if he paid me fifty times more.'

'This is a very crazy thing you say.'

'When you don't have much longer to live,' I said, 'you can afford to be crazy. Now,' I added, 'you either call Danny from here or go back to him and tell him that I must talk to him, in person, before I die — which could be within a few months. Then and only then will I decide whether or not to help him out.'

She nodded grudgingly, turned and started toward the door.

'One last thing,' I said, stopping her. 'Tell him this too: that if he's mixed up with LaSalle, or works for him as a pusher or a dealer, then he's crossed the line as far as I'm concerned and I want no part of him. Got that?'

Alita nodded. I opened the door for her. She stepped out into the hall, started away then stopped and came back and looked at me, long and hard before saying: 'Now I will tell you something. Danny is not any of those things you say — '

'Then why is LaSalle after him?'

'For destroying Julien's last shipment of heroin from Afghanistan.'

'Destroying it?'

'Yes. It had just been unloaded from a ship and stored in one of Julien's warehouses on the docks. Danny set fire to it. The warehouse burned down and everything was lost in the fire.'

Knowing my brother and how selfish and uncaring he could be, it was a hard story to swallow. Alita read my expression and said: 'Danny said you would not believe he did this . . . that's why he didn't want me to tell you.'

'Well, you know what they say about leopards and spots,' I said. 'My brother's a classic example.'

Alita turned and walked off without another word.

'Have him call me or meet me somewhere,' I called after her. 'It's the only way he'll get his money.'

She ignored me and continued on to the elevator. There, she punched the button and while waiting for the car to arrive, took out her cell and called someone.

I hoped it was Danny.

14

Alone in my suite, I fixed myself a martini and went out on the balcony to relax and enjoy it. But I had so many conflicting thoughts racing around in my head, it was impossible. Mind churning, I stared out at the dark choppy waters of the Mediterranean, trying to figure out whether Alita or Michelle, Inspector Bonfils and the others were telling me the truth — or if either side was.

One thing was certain though — no matter who was lying, or why, I knew that Danny was somehow involved; and if I wanted to talk to him and straighten out our differences I'd better find him before LaSalle's men did . . . or I might wind up talking to a corpse.

The ringing of the phone interrupted my thoughts. I hurried inside and answered it. It was Kirk, anxious to tell me that according to his sources in Paris and Nice, Danny had managed to steal a shipment of heroin that was on its way to LaSalle and was now trying to sell it on the open market.

'That's not the way I heard it,' I said, and then related what Alita had just told me.

Kirk wasn't impressed. 'My people are pretty damned reliable, Irish. And let's face it. The Danny we both know would never pass up a chance to make a few million bucks, especially just to be noble. I mean it's totally out of character.'

I had to agree with him. 'Well, we'll soon know,' I said. 'Alita's supposed to get back to me right after she's given Danny my ultimatum. And if he accepts my offer — and I've never known my brother to turn down free money — I'm sure I'll be meeting with him sometime tomorrow.'

Kirk gave an irritated sigh. 'Fine,' he said sharply. 'Call me the second you hear from him, okay?'

I promised I would and hung up. Suddenly very tired, I took a long hot bath, fixed myself a nightcap and went to bed. I was exhausted, but sleep eluded me. I couldn't stop thinking about Danny or who, if anyone, I should trust. It was almost dawn before I finally drifted off.

Then, what seemed like moments later but according to the bedside clock was actually two hours, the jangling phone awoke me with a start. I groped for the receiver, fumbling it off the hook and saying: ''Lo?'

'Sis, it's me.'

It was the first time in several months that I'd talked to my brother and for a moment my sleep-deadened brain didn't respond.

'Jackie — it's Danny — can you hear me?'

'Y-Yeah,' I said, yawning. 'I hear you. Where are you? Are you all right?'

'I'm fine. Just fine. Alita told me what you said — '

'Do you believe me?'

'Yes. Listen, sis, I've got to see you right away.'

'Tell me where you are. I'll be there soon as I get dressed.'

'Not on the phone. But Alita's waiting for you outside — across from the hotel

— on the grass facing the fountain. She'll take you to me.' The line went dead.

Jumping out of bed, I threw on some clothes, grabbed my purse and hurried out.

★ ★ ★

The *Place du Casino*, a large open square fronting my hotel, the Casino and other surrounding buildings, was almost deserted at that gray pre-dawn hour. I stopped on the top of the entrance steps and looked around for any signs of danger. Several workers were washing down the sidewalk and streets with hoses, and a few cars raced past along the sea-front highway but otherwise the area was empty.

I stood there another moment, a chilly breeze off the Mediterranean making me shiver, and then spotted someone standing on the other side of the low, circular grassy mound facing the hotel. The street lights were still on, but I couldn't see the person's face. It was definitely a woman though and guessing it was Alita, I descended the steps and crossed over toward her.

As I approached, she must have heard my heels clicking on the street because she turned and faced me. She smiled as she recognized me and waved. Relieved, I continued walking toward her. Her hand now dipped into the pocket of her coat and as I came up to her I saw the tell-tale bulge of a gun. For an instant I panicked and considered trying to run. But there was no cover other than a few vehicles parked across the street, and knowing she could easily shoot me before I got very far, I pretended nothing was wrong. Besides, she was still smiling. So fighting down my fears I stopped in front of her and asked where Danny was.

'In the van behind me,' she replied. '*Allez . . .* ' We started walking.

It was then I noticed the unmarked brown van parked a few yards away. The engine was still running and a man in a dark-blue beret and a gabardine raincoat was hunched over the wheel. He glanced my way and I immediately recognized him: it was the older of the two detectives who'd questioned Kirk and me in my hotel room. Remembering what Kirk had said about him, I suddenly felt uneasy.

'Wait a minute,' I said, stopping. 'Before I go another step I want to see my brother.'

Alita turned to me and said angrily: 'If Danny shows his face out here, he could be killed.' She looked nervously around, her eyes searching the parked vehicles, rooftops and side-streets leading away from the square. 'Is that what you want?'

''Course not.'

'Then do not doubt me.'

'Why shouldn't I? You've had a gun on me ever since I left the hotel.'

'It's not for you,' she said, again looking nervously about her. 'It is for your brother's protection. Even as we talk, there may be snipers waiting for a chance to shoot him. Now, hurry . . . ' Before I could argue, she grasped my arm and started pulling me toward the van.

As we came up to the van the side door slid open and there, half-standing, half-hunkered over, was my kid brother!

'Danny!' I exclaimed and started to climb into the van.

I expected him to greet me with open

arms and a big smile. Instead, he looked guilty, almost frightened, and as I got closer, he suddenly waved his arms for me to get back and yelled: 'No! Get away, sis! Run! Ru — '

It was then a man who'd been crouching behind him knocked Danny aside and stood up, and covered me with a machine pistol. At the same time the older detective swung his seat around and covered me with his handgun.

I froze, stunned, and felt Alita jab me in the back with her gun.

'Get inside,' she began — and then stopped, gasping in pain as a shot rang out from one of the parked cars. She dropped her gun, the .45 semi-automatic falling at my feet, and collapsed without another word.

A lot of things happened at once after that:

Inside the van my brother whirled around and kicked the machine pistol out of the crouching man's hands — the older detective shot Danny, causing him to grunt painfully and drop to his knees — I grabbed up Alita's gun and fired several shots at the older detective, who slumped over and then slid to the floor — and finally several shadowy figures came running up, surrounding the van. They were all armed and pushing me aside, aimed their weapons at the crouching man just as he was picking up his machine pistol.

They didn't give him a chance to surrender: they all fired at him, their bullets punching him backward so that he slammed against the wall of the van and then fell forward, already dead as he sprawled on the floor.

It had all happened so fast I didn't really see the faces of the men who were gathered around me. Now, as rushed forward in an effort to reach my wounded brother, two of them held me back while a third man confronted me, saying: '*Se calmer, se calmer* . . . Please, Ms. O'Hara . . . calm down.'

It was Bonfils. Fighting to break loose from the two men, I yelled: 'Inspector! Make them let me go! H-He's hurt . . . Danny . . . my brother . . . he was shot and — '

'It's all right,' Michelle said, joining us. 'I've already called for an ambulance . . . Danny will be fine, Jackie. I promise . . . '

Another man came pushing up. Recognizing the Interpol agent Mike Flynn, I realized I was in safe company. 'Please,' I begged Michelle. 'Let me talk to Danny.'

She nodded and the men holding me released my arms. I pushed past her and saw another man helping Danny down from the van. He'd been shot in the right arm and blood was already staining the sleeve of his jacket.

Seeing me, he gave a rueful, painful smile. 'Hi, sis . . . '

'You okay?'

'Sure.' He looked at the two dead bodies in the van and then at Alita's bloodied corpse lying in the street. 'Man, I sure screwed things up, didn't I?'

'Doesn't matter,' I said, gratefully. 'All that matters is you're safe.'

'Yeah, thanks to her,' he said, looking at Michelle. She smiled at him and I saw genuine affection in her eyes. 'She saved my neck in Cannes and now, here . . . '

He paused and smiled at her, adding: 'I don't know why you did it . . . or even bothered with me at all, but . . . thank God you did.'

She stepped close to him and gently kissed him on the cheek. 'When you are well, *mon bon ami*, I will tell you.' Then to me: 'Your brother is very brave. Not only did he destroy most of LaSalle's heroin supply, he helped us draw him out of Cannes so we could pin murder and drug charges on him.'

'That's Julien LaSalle?' I said, pointing at the corpse in the van.

'No — his top lieutenant, Jean-Louis Richard. But we have LaSalle trapped in a villa not far from here. Unless he shoots himself, which isn't likely, we'll take him alive and he will die in prison.'

'What about her?' I said, pointing at Alita's corpse. 'Where's she fit into all this?'

'She worked for LaSalle, doing anything he asked. He knew Danny trusted her and thought she had the best chance of finding him.'

I shook my head, still a bit confused. 'I have to tell you, Michelle, for a while there I wasn't sure whom I could trust.'

She smiled. 'Believe me, there were times I wasn't sure myself.'

In the distance I could hear the discordant wail of an approaching ambulance. Smiling at Danny, I helped him take off his jacket and sit on the edge of the van floor.

'I'm so proud of you,' I said, squeezing his hand.

'Don't be,' he replied, his voice filled with regret. 'I don't deserve you, sis. Never have. Why the hell you've stuck by me, God only knows.'

'Shhhh,' I whispered. 'We'll talk about all that after they fix up your arm.'

He nodded, looked at his bloody sleeve then back at me. 'I've got to know something, sis — is it true? Are you really . . . I mean . . . ?' He lowered his eyes, unable to finish.

I leaned forward, kissed him on the forehead and then sat beside him.

'We'll talk about that later, too.'

The ambulance was close now. The onlookers who'd gathered were being ordered to stand back by the *gendarmes* and I could see flashing roof-lights approaching.

'I love you,' I said softly to Danny. 'More than anything. You know that, don't you?'

As if I hadn't spoken, he said urgently: 'You're not going to die, sis. I won't let you. I need you. Always have . . . ' He broke off, tears running down his cheeks.

I put my arm about his waist and kept it there, wishing as I did that he was right: that somehow I wouldn't die . . . at least, not for a long, long time.

15

I sat with Danny in the emergency hospital while a doctor patched him up. The bullet had gone clean through his arm so surgery wasn't necessary. But he was weak from loss of blood, so I insisted they keep him overnight.

With the help of Michelle and Inspector Bonfils I also got the local police to assign one of their men to guard him twenty-four-seven — just in case the Russian Mafia got wind of my brother's whereabouts and sent one of their hit men to take him out.

I paid to have an extra bed put in Danny's room and never left his side. Maybe because he'd been shot, or that we both knew from now on every minute we spent together was precious — whatever the reason, I'd never felt more close to him. And if I'm to believe what he told me during our many intimate conversations, it was the same with him.

The hardest, most painful part was telling him about my chronic leukemia and that I only had a year at most to live.

'I don't believe that,' he said adamantly. 'I won't believe it. Ever! This is 2012, for God's sake. There's got to be something the doctors can do about it. I know there is, sis.'

'Let's hope you're right,' I said as cheerfully as I could. 'I sure as hell don't want to give up living; especially now that we're finally together again. Speaking of which,' I added, 'did Michelle or Mike Flynn mention anything about when you'd be extradited back to New York?'

'Not yet, no.' He gave a sour laugh. 'Too bad I'm not a murderer — France doesn't extradite defendants to countries that have the death penalty. It's okay, though,' he added before I could reply. 'I've given it a lot of thought lately and I've decided to go home and be a witness for the D.A. — '

'No, you can't! That bastard Kaslov will have you killed.'

'He'll try, I know, sis. But, hey, you think he's going to just sit idly by while I enjoy my days here or in some other foreign country? I don't think so. As long as I'm alive he knows my testimony could put him in the chair, and he's not going to be cool with that.'

'But what about us? We've only got a short time together as it is. I don't want to shorten it even more because some low-life Russian mobster decides to have you killed.'

'Neither do I, sis. But if I don't put Kaslov away for good, it'll only be a matter of time before one of his cretins gets to me. And I don't want to spend the rest of my life — or yours — hiding out. I've done that and it sucks. From now on, once the trial's over, we're going to have nothing but fun together.'

He was right and I knew it. 'Fair enough,' I said. I gently hugged him and then got out my BlackBerry and texted Kirk that I'd found Danny and would be bringing him home in a day or two.

He responded almost immediately. 'Miranda and I will join you tomorrow morning. Then we can all fly home together. Love, Kirk.'

I showed Danny the text message.

'Who's Miranda?' he asked. 'His private secretary?'

'Uh-uh. His private jet,' I said. 'Kirk named it after the Flying Fortress his grandfather flew during World War Two.'

Danny looked surprised. 'I didn't know Kirk's grandpa was a pilot. I mean he never talks about him. Least, not to me.'

'Maybe that's because, right from the start you made it clear that you didn't want anything to do with him. And that's too bad, because for all his faults Kirk's a really good guy who could've helped you through the bad times.'

Danny nodded and mulled things over for a moment. Then he said quietly: 'You're right, sis. I didn't give him a chance.' He sighed, troubled by his thoughts. 'Guess I was too busy being jealous of him — you know, for coming into our lives, marrying you and . . . taking you away from me.'

'He never took me away from you, Danny. That was all in your mind. Kirk may have entered our lives — mine especially — but he never tried to exclude you or get between us. Quite the opposite: he always tried to *include* you in whatever we were doing. So did I. I was always there for you. And always will be.'

Danny didn't say anything for several moments. Then, out of the blue, he said: 'I haven't done any drugs for two, almost three months now. And hopefully I won't ever again.'

I smiled, relieved. 'That's the best news you've ever given me.'

As if I hadn't spoken, he said: 'You still love him, don't you — Kirk, I mean?'

I nodded.

'And I know he loves you. So why don't you guys — '

'Get married again?' I said, cutting him off. 'That's simple. Because we love each other more when we're not married. Sounds crazy I know. But it's a fact and both of us have come to accept it — even if it's not what we really want.'

Danny absorbed my words, his mind awhirl with thoughts. Then suddenly he smiled like a kid on Christmas morning. 'Miranda,' he said, amused. 'That's sure a weird name to call an airplane; especially a bomber.'

'I think it's romantic,' I said.

'That's 'cause you're a girl and girls think everything's romantic.'

'I think it's romantic,' I repeated, ignoring his comment, 'because Miranda was the name of Grandpa Harmon's wife. It was painted on the fuselage of his B17. And every time just before they took off on a mission, grandpa and the whole crew would kiss their fingertips and then pat the name for good luck. They flew forty missions over Germany and never even got as much as a scratch. Nobody could explain it. But Grandpa Harmon swore to the day he passed that it was Miranda that kept them from being shot down. Said she was looking after them and . . . '

I stopped as I realized Danny wasn't listening. He'd dozed off while I'd been talking. Rising, I bent over him, pulled the blanket up under his chin and kissed him lightly on the forehead.

It was probably the mother instinct in me, but it felt so good to be looking after my kid brother again. And though there was no way of telling how long we'd be together, of one thing I was sure. Now that we'd found each other again, Danny and I were going to make that reunion last just as long as we possibly could.

THE END

We do hope that you have enjoyed reading this large print book.

Did you know that all of our titles are available for purchase?

We publish a wide range of high quality large print books including:

Romances, Mysteries, Classics
General Fiction
Non Fiction and Westerns

Special interest titles available in large print are:

The Little Oxford Dictionary
Music Book, Song Book
Hymn Book, Service Book

Also available from us courtesy of Oxford University Press:

Young Readers' Dictionary
(large print edition)
Young Readers' Thesaurus
(large print edition)

For further information or a free brochure, please contact us at:
Ulverscroft Large Print Books Ltd.,
The Green, Bradgate Road, Anstey,
Leicester, LE7 7FU, England.
Tel: (00 44) **0116 236 4325**
Fax: (00 44) **0116 234 0205**

VICTORIAN VILLAINY

Michael Kurland

Professor James Moriarty stands alone as the particular nemesis of Sherlock Holmes. But just how evil was he? Here are four ingenious stories, all exploring an alternate possibility: that Moriarty wasn't really a villain at all. But why, then, did Holmes describe Moriarty as 'the greatest schemer of all time', and 'the Napoleon of crime'? Holmes could never *catch* Moriarty in any of his imagined schemes — which only reinforced his conviction that the professor was, indeed, an evil genius . . .

THE DYRYSGOL HORROR AND OTHER STORIES

Edmund Glasby

What is the nature of the evil that terrorises Dyrysgol? Detective Inspector Bernard Owen's investigation involves people disappearing from this remote Welsh village. Local anger is directed towards Dyrysgol Castle and its enigmatic owner. But whilst Viscount Ravenwood is a little strange, is he a murderer? Then another man goes missing and his car is left with great claw marks across the roof, as Owen and his officers are dragged towards the bloody conclusion of the mystery of Dyrysgol . . .